About the Author

Trevor Few lives in the Hertfordshire town of Hemel Hempstead and has worked for many years writing technical manuals for the aircraft industry. When not working, he likes to potter about in his garden or walk the Cornish coastal paths. Now, in his middle age, he is spending his midlife crisis writing works of fiction.

I hope you
enjoy.

Trevor Few

Di-Ablo's Revenge

Trevor Few

Di-Ablo's Revenge

Olympia Publishers
London

www.olympiapublishers.com
OLYMPIA PAPERBACK EDITION

A CIP catalogue record for this title is
available from the British Library.

ISBN: 978-1-80439-392-5

This is a work of fiction.
Names, characters, places and incidents originate from the writer's
imagination. Any resemblance to actual persons, living or dead, is
purely coincidental.

First Published in 2023

Olympia Publishers
Tallis House
2 Tallis Street
London
EC4Y 0AB

Printed in Great Britain

Dedication

I dedicate this book to my wife, Yvonne, and all my friends and family that have helped and supported me during the writing of this book.

Acknowledgements

Thank you to my wife, Yvonne, for encouraging me to write this book.

Chapter One

Mother Evandoria looked at the stragglers who were making their way into the stone circle and then at her watch. It was eleven forty-five, fifteen minutes before the appointed hour, enough time to get the ceremony underway. Tonight was an important night; it was the night they would summon their master from his realm into theirs and free him from his unearthly incarceration to once again walk upon the earth. Well that was the plan according to the text she had received a few days ago from an untraceable phone number that has a lot of sixes in it.

She looked at the now fully assembled coven of witches that stood before her. All were dressed in their blackest of robes, all of which had been specially washed and pressed for the occasion. Faces obscured by shadowy hoods, each held a flaming flambeau giving the obligatory eerie flickering glow to the proceedings.

"Ladies, it is good to see you all managed to make it here on time and I apologise for the short notice, but our master does not work to earthly time scales, his ways are beyond comprehension. Now, is everyone here?"

A murmur ran around the group followed by a louder but still timid voice from somewhere near the back of the crowd.

"Not quite. Muriel couldn't make it her Colin's back is playing up again and she promised to put a poultice on it tonight."

"No matter, we are strong; we can summon our master without the aid of Sister Muriel." So saying she turned and with a flourish plunged her flambeau into a brazier containing dry straw and wood that had been seasoned with a generous sprinkling of lighter fluid. The contents ignited with a whoosh and added their own ethereal glow to the proceedings. The fire was not strictly necessary for the ceremony but her eyes were not as good as they used to be and the ground was uneven and damp, and tripping over her own feet in the dark was something she wanted to avoid on this the most special of nights.

"Is the sacrifice ready?"

A robed figure stepped out of the semi gloom and into the glow of the firelight. It stopped in front of mother Evandoria, bowed its head and held the offering in outstretched arms.

Mother Evandoria peered at the offering held in the outspread hands, not quite understanding what she was seeing. She looked at the assembled group, all with their heads bowed in silent reverence, and then back at the offering. In a low whispered hiss she rebuked the figure bowing in front of her.

"What is this? I distinctly told you to bring a lamb's heart for the ritual." She prodded the offering with a finger. "What is this? Sausages! You brought sausages. Tonight of all nights!"

The outstretched arms started to tremble slightly.

"Yes, o' Powerful Mother. I am sorry, you see I was a bit late back from the school run and the butcher was just closing up for the day and this is all he had available. They are his special vegetarian sausages – I've had them before, they are very nice."

Mother Evandoria could feel her blood pressure go up a point or two.

"Vegetarian sausages for a sacrifice, did you not stop to think…" The arms trembled a little more.

"Sorry. I just thought it might be a nice change, and after the ceremony we could cook them over the fire to warm us up a bit. I have some nice seed topped bread rolls in my bag to go with them."

In all her years she had never heard anything quite like it. She blamed the younger incomers to the village with their modern ways and she questioned their commitment to the cause.

They were witches with a proud heritage going back hundreds if not thousands of years, not a branch of the WI out on a picnic.

Time was getting on and strictly a sacrifice was not really necessary, it was more of an expectation, something to get the assembled mob in the right mood. She took the sacrificial sausages, held them up to the sky and then laid them on the altar stone, picked up a knife in both hands and held it up high for all the crowd to see. Slowly she started to recite the ancient sacred incantation that had been handed down through the generations. She had recited it many times through her witching career and knew it off by heart. She may have been able to recite it verbatim but she did not know what it meant. Once in an idle moment she had put it through an online translator and came up with an old recipe for crab apple jelly, but she thought that was just another conspiracy by those shadowy people that run the internet to conceal the truth from the masses. Finishing the chant she plunged the knife into the pile of vegetarian sausages.

For a few moments there was a deathly silence, nothing stirred, even the flames stopped flickering as time itself seemed to stand still. Then suddenly without warning there was a buzzing of static electricity and greenish blue sparks started to ark across the two largest stones in the circle. The intensity of the buzzing grew stronger and stronger until the witches could bear it no more; some ran away in fear while others covered their ears in a futile attempt to stop it eating into their brains. Just as it was becoming intolerable a large blue flash darted out from the tallest stone up into the night sky, momentarily illuminating the area as if it were a bright summer's day. As the sky dimmed once more into darkness and the accompanying sonic boom reverberating through the hills died away, a door slowly faded into existence between the two large upright stones of the circle.

It was a good solid oak door of gothic design complete with sturdy steel hinges and iron studs that had materialised in the stone circle. The witches stood and looked at the door in silent amazement at first, but this amazement turned a little more to fear as the large iron doorknob rattled and the door creaked on its hinges as it slowly opened.

"Good morning, ladies. I am glad to see you got my message."

The witches looked at the tall muscular figure who had walked through the door and dropped to their knees, heads bowed. Mother Evandoria, kneeling in the damp grass with her head bowed in deference, spoke to the entity that stood before them, his large frame silhouetted against the pale orange light that seeped through the open doorway. "We are honoured by your presence mighty master."

He gazed down on the prostrate figures of the witches and was pleased with what he saw. Punctuality and blind obedience were the two main traits he looked for in his subjects.

"It is good to be here. Most of you will know who I am but for any newcomers here tonight my name is Vyncent Di-Ablo, harbinger of plague and pestilence. If you want crops withered or an enemy taken care of, I am your man. My friends – and I feel I am amongst friends here – call me Vynce. Now please stand, all of you, so we can get to know each other a little bit better."

The news that they could stand came as a relief to Mother Evandoria as kneeling in the damp grass was playing havoc with her arthritic knees. Rising unsteadily to her feet she stood up and stuck her hand out in the familiar greeting.

"It is good to have you here, Mast... er, Vynce. We have heard many tales of your misdeeds over the centuries. Please let me introduce you to the girls."

Vynce took the proffered hand and shook it.

"That would be splendid." As he spoke his eyes were drawn to the offering that lay on the altar stone. "Are they sausages? Did you use sausages in the sacred ritual?"

"Yes, Master, they were all we could get at short notice."

"Splendid use of initiative, pop them over the fire, I'm starving."

"I am afraid they are vegetarian."

Vynce took a long cold hard look at the sausages and then back at the witch and a big grin spread across his face.

"Nasty things vegetarian sausages, quite evil in fact. Did anyone think to bring any bread rolls?"

Chapter Two

It was a pleasantly mild late summer/early autumn evening although the air was beginning to chill a little as the sun started to sink below the horizon. A celebration was in full swing at Rose Well Farm. An accordion player played local folk songs competing with an ever-rising level of cider fuelled revelry while the smell of barbeque wafted tantalisingly on the breeze. The party was to celebrate the successful gathering in of the harvest and to thank the staff for their hard work over the year. It was something that Freddy and Sally had started when they took over the farm and was now an annual event which was firmly fixed in the farm calendar.

Wine glass in hand, Sally sat down on a straw bale and looked out over the fields in the gathering dusk and felt a sense of pride and purpose. Her farm was helping to keep the nation fed as well as being a source of employment for the village which in turn helped to keep the local economy alive. Also the introduction of solar panels onto the barn roofs and the purchase of battery powered farm equipment meant that they were almost carbon neutral. If only they could do something about the flatulence of the farm animals then they could truly claim to be fully carbon neutral and, just as importantly, methane neutral.

Her thoughts were interrupted as she felt someone sit down beside her. She looked up to see Ted the farm manager manoeuvring himself down onto the bale. He had a pint pot of the county's finest cloudy scrumpy in his hand and she could tell by his demeanour and breath it was not his first of the night.

"I would just like to say on behalf of myself and the rest of the staff, thank you Sally for this wonderful celebration."

She turned slightly to face him and smiled. The scrumpy had thickened his West Country drawl and he was slurring his words slightly. He was an honest, hardworking man and she knew that without his hard work and encyclopaedic knowledge of all things agricultural the farm would not be the success that it was.

"Thank you, Ted, it is just a token to show our appreciation of all your hard work throughout the year."

Ted raised his pint pot. "I'll drink to that."

Sally raised her wine glass and chinked it against his pint pot.

After a moments' silence she stood up and started to make her way back to where the party was in full swing. As she moved, something in the corner of her eye caught her attention and she turned to get a better look. There it was a dull orange glow out towards the edge of the village.

"Ted. Do you know if there are any other celebrations in the village tonight? It looks like they are lighting the beacon over there on Hogsback Tor."

He rose unsteadily to his feet to get a better view.

"No. Not that I am aware of, besides the beacon is a bit more over there to the left. That looks more like the direction of that new mobile phone mast they put up near High Meadow Manor."

He fished a battered old mobile phone out of his pocket, flipped it open and stabbed at the buttons with his fingers. It might have been old but it was reliable. Many a time he had fished it out of the muck spreader and hosed it down, but it had always come good. His network provider had sent him some flyers a while back trying to get him to purchase a new all singing and dancing smart phone for a modest rise in his monthly fee, but he had thrown them on the fire. What did he need the internet for? He knew all he needed to know about farming and where to go to get a decent cider and he certainly had no interest in looking at pictures of other people's dinner which from his limited experience seemed to be the mainstay of social media sites. No, he was happy with what he had.

"No signal. The network is down; it must be the mast on fire, probably overloaded with all them selfies with the cows that them townies send to each other after a day in the country."

On the outskirts of the village not far from the beacon on Hogsback Tor, a group of shadowy figures dressed in neatly pressed black robes assembled in the gathering darkness by the recently installed mobile phone mast. One of the robed figures stepped forward and waved their arms at the crowd in an appeal for attention.

"Can I have your attention please, ladies? You know why we are here tonight." There was a shuffling from the back of the crowd.

"Yes. We are here to take out this instrument of deep state and corporate manipulation and prevent them from beaming mind-altering subliminal thoughts directly into our brains."

Sensing that the rest of the mob was getting restless, the leader waved her arms in a palm down expression in an appeal for calm.

"No! That that is certainly not why we are here."

Another dissenting voice piped up. "I am sure it is. I heard from a friend's mate who knew someone that had seen it on social media that they are using the latest mobile technology to beam various things like tracking chips and viruses directly into the bodies of the local population in order to subdue the masses and generally manipulate their lives and stuff. It's true, they have done the research!"

The mob leader shook her head in disbelief.

"NO! That is not it at all. Surely you can see that all that is just fairy tales put around by people who have nothing better to do. Think about it, if it was possible to beam thoughts or tracking chips and the like into our bodies that would mean that they have invented some sort of teleport device. Do you really think they would use such a device in that way?

"Wouldn't a better use of such technology be to generate big money for corporations by charging extortionately high fees to beam businessmen and world leaders across the globe to meetings thus saving time and energy? NO, we are here at the request of our master Vynce Di-Ablo to place this bugging device in the workings of this perfectly ordinary phone mast so that he can eavesdrop on his business rivals and intercept their messages and data."

This did nothing to calm the mood of the mob.

"I don't believe you. It was on social media so it must be true. You are just as bad as they are, standing there trying to fool us with your facts and science. I reckon you are part of the deep state conspiracy trying to hide the truth from us, the masses."

A roar of agreement ran around the assembled crowd and the mob surged forward, pushing Mother Evandoria aside. Someone produced bolt cutters and they cut their way through the flimsy chain link fence that surrounded the mast and then sprinkled a liberal dose of petrol over the control boxes at its base. After retreating to a safe distance a rag was stuffed into a bottle of petrol, set alight and then thrown at the mobile phone mast. There was a whoosh as the petrol vapour ignited and engulfed the mast in flames.

It was a fine sunny morning as Sally cycled down the lane and into the village. She needed a loaf of bread and was headed for the village bakery where they did a rather nice uncut farmhouse loaf. It was nice to be out in the fresh air feeling the sun on her face. Cycling was something she had recently taken up in an effort to get more exercise and be a little greener by leaving the car at home and using it only when necessary. She also had a bit of a thick head from the previous night's revelry and thought the exercise might help to clear it a little.

As she neared the village the air became decidedly less fresh and a distinct smell of burnt chemicals and plastic filled her nostrils. The phone mast was a little way outside the village and the fire was long since out but the smell of the previous night's inferno hung in the air like an unwanted guest. Coughing slightly as the tainted air entered her lungs, she stopped outside the bakery, got off her bike, propped it against the wall and entered the shop.

"Hello, Sally, the usual uncut farmhouse, is it?"

"Yes please, Mrs Drimpton. Is something burning out there? Only there is a nasty smell of melted plastic in the air today."

Mrs Drimpton shuffled her feet uncomfortably and set the loaf down on the counter. She was a long standing member of the coven and had been there at the previous night's debacle. She had not taken part directly herself and being of modest upbringing had not understood most of what was said about deep state interference and microchips, but still felt a little guilty nonetheless at what had happened and put the blame on the younger, more volatile members of the group. Hopefully the power and anonymity of the coven would protect her from any repercussions.

"Have you not heard? That new phone mast they put up near the manor house was burned down last night. It's caused havoc, most of the village is without a signal. No social media or anything like that on your phone round here now. I hear tempers are wearing thin as people are now having to talk to each other face to face rather than communicate by text."

Sally paid for her loaf and waited for her change.

"That makes sense. I thought I saw flames last night. Ted said he thought it might be the phone mast but he had had a few so I didn't take much notice. Who do you think would do a thing like that?"

Mrs Drimpton handed Sally her change.

"Probably kids from the town, you know what they're like. Ted said he had a good time at your harvest do last night when he came in to pick up his pasty this morning. Mind you he still looked a little worse for wear, so I should keep him away from any heavy machinery if I were you."

Outside the shop curiosity was getting the better of her, and the phone mast was only a short cycle ride away. Stowing the bread safely in the cycle's front basket she got back on and headed in the direction of the manor. As she neared the site of the previous night's conflagration the smell of burnt plastic became stronger and she could see dampness in the side of the road where the water from the fire hoses had run down the slight incline and formed pools before draining away. Up ahead she could see the charred and distorted remains of the mast which now looked to be leaning precariously from about halfway up.

The heat from the fire had been so hot that the metal had buckled and bent. Leaning her bike against the hedge, she walked over to where the local community police officer was busy securing the area with blue and white striped plastic tape.

"It looks a mess. Was it an accident? Rumour in the village is that it was done on purpose."

He tied off the last piece of tape and looked up at Sally. He prided himself on knowing everyone in the village. Most of the families in the village had lived and worked there for hundreds of years. On this scale Sally was a relative newcomer and in his view should be treated with suspicion. He had heard stories of strange exotic plants being grown in the conservatory up at the farm and was looking for a good excuse to go and investigate.

"I am not at liberty to say, ma'am, but I have been asked to cordon it off for the fire investigation team, so take that as you will."

Sally looked at the twisted metal and melted plastic and thought it reminded her of a painting of melting clocks by one of those surrealist painters she had once seen in a magazine.

"It is a shame; we were just getting used to having a reliable mobile phone signal. I guess I will just have to go back to the old way of standing on a chair in the middle of the stable yard to get a strong enough signal to make a call or send a text."

He placed the roll of tape on the ground, stood back and admired his handiwork.

"You are not the only one. I hear the new owner of the manor is not best pleased either I believe he was relying on this installation to give him some sort of fast communication link for his business, came down here personally this morning to take a look on his way out to town."

Sally made her excuses and pulled her bike out of the hedge. She was just about to get back on it when a car came around the corner. It was a brand new shiny black Bentley Continental with a custom paint job of hot rod flames extending out from the front wheel arches and over the doors. It looked to be driven by a very small chauffer who was having difficulty seeing over the steering wheel. The passenger in the back looked vaguely familiar. As it passed by she saw the private plate number 'D1 ABL0' and she felt an icy cold finger of fear run down her spine. The car turned and headed up the long drive to the manor house.

Vynce Di-Ablo sat behind his large and expensive desk and listened in disbelief to the tale being told to him by Mother Evandoria.

"Have I got this right, Ms Evandoria – can I call you Dora?"

She nodded.

"Thank you, Dora. You are telling me that you somehow allowed the women of your coven to get out of control and burn down the phone mast I had asked you to bug, all because of some unsubstantiated conspiracy theory that is doing the rounds on the web. Do you know how many palms I had to grease to get that mast put in the village especially so I could eavesdrop on my competitors?"

Dora shifted uneasily in her chair.

"Sorry, Master. I blame the internet; it is now so easy to disseminate false information to the masses, it is difficult to compete. In the old days it took time, first you needed to create a cult (such as ours), then lure members in, isolate them from their families, and then brain wash them into your particular point of view. Now all you need is a cyber presence on social media, then create a semi reasonable argument that hooks in the gullible and do all the indoctrination online. It is so much easier and cheaper. We are struggling to get our particular message out there now. I have it on good authority that some of the elders are seriously considering setting up an online presence just so as we can get our voices heard."

Vynce considered the words of the village wise woman and found on balance she was probably right. He had been away a while and all things technological had moved forward at quite a pace. Perhaps he should look at moving with the times and also set up an online presence to help in his quest for world domination, but for now he required a solution to his predicament. Without an operational phone mast he needed some other way of eavesdropping on his competition.

"You may be right, but that doesn't help me at the moment. I still need to spy on my rivals. A thought occurs to me, do you still have that crystal ball?"

Chapter Three

They looked in dismay at the screens in front of them, the head of security tapped away on his keyboard. Nothing changed, the screens still showed the same black and white snowy static and white noise hissed out from the speakers, the same as all the other times they had reviewed the CCTV footage from the previous night.

The site operations manager looked at the head of security in disbelief.

"How could this happen, Mike? This is a top secret facility with the latest advances in security systems and someone just walks in and helps themselves to our entire stock of a highly restricted nerve agent and then walks back out without leaving a trace, no surveillance footage, no finger prints, no usable DNA – nothing?"

Mike had been head of security at the facility for many years, working his way up through the system, starting in the military police before specialising in security for highly sensitive applications such as this and was proud of his record to date. In his time there had not been any breaches of security and certainly no thefts. His staff had even dealt swiftly and severely last year with those two young boys who had come up to the main gate asking if they could come in and capture the mythical creature from their interactive computer game that was alleged to be found at a grid reference that fell within boundaries of the facility. Those were the good old days, but unfortunately today was a bad day, his career was over. Who would employ him once it got out what had happened last night on his watch? He put on a brave face.

"It has got to be a state actor to get past our security and then make their way straight to the lab's storage facility. They seemed to know exactly what they wanted and where to find it. There must have also been some form of inside knowledge."

The site operations manager nodded. Something strange had happened last night but he did not think it was state sponsored. He knew for a fact that the formula for that particular nerve agent had been leaked to the country's enemies and friends alike some years ago in a clandestine operation to discredit a certain regime that would remain anonymous. Any state could make it if they so desired, besides it wasn't even that effective, at worst it only disorientated you for a few minutes and then left you with hangover-like symptoms, in his experience a bit like a good Saturday night out on the town. Why steal it? Although it was not very good as a chemical weapon, if this substance was to get into the wrong hands it would have a catastrophic impact on those that came in contact with it, so they needed to get it back and fast.

"How did they get past the main gate?"

"According to Stan who was on duty last night, the last thing he remembers is a battered old removals van pulling up to the main gate where a small wizened old man holding an old fashioned candle lamp in his hand got out and started to talk to him. He remembers feeling a compulsion to follow the man. Then the rest is a blank until he wakes up in a field full of cabbages five miles from the site completely disorientated. I think the lamp must have been giving off some sort of fumes that rendered him unconscious and they dumped him in the field as they left."

"I see. Even then, how did they manage to get past all the high tech reinforced doors without a pass key or setting off the alarms?"

Mike could feel his palms getting sweaty.

"The alarms we are not sure about, some sort of jamming signal perhaps, but the doors... Well, they were ripped to matchwood. We don't know how they did it as they are designed to withstand attack by explosives, but somehow they managed to rip them off their hinges and leave them in splinters – even the bullet proof glass panels were completely smashed."

The operations manager nodded again and looked at his watch.

"OK. I have to go and brief the minister now but if you could put all this in a written report and have it on my desk in an hour that would be appreciated."

Mike nodded his assent and made a mental note to call in on the job centre on his way home to see what was on offer in the way of an alternative career. If he was lucky and they gave him a reasonable reference he might still be able to get a position as a store detective.

Outside a barn in a remote part of High Meadow Manor small figures in white lab coats, wearing respirators and chemical proof gloves, were busy organising the unloading of the cargo from a battered old removal van that had seen better days. Most of the hard work of removing the large drums from the van and placing them in the barn was being done by a large troll called Terrence.

No one knew how to correctly pronounce his real name in the troll dialect, so over time he had gained the nickname Terrence the troll which had for convenience then just been shortened to Terrence. Terrence had only been working at the manor for a couple of weeks but was finding it a fulfilling career move. Most of the work involved any heavy lifting that was required, for which he got in return three good meals a day and his own barn to sleep in. As if this was not reward enough he also had the pleasure of patrolling the estate at night frightening off any unwanted visitors such as poachers that may be foolish enough to trespass on the grounds of High Meadow Manor.

Last night though had been the pinnacle of his career so far when he had smashed his way into the lab facility and helped to remove the contents from the secure store. Still feeling the exhilaration from the night before, it was with a smile on his face and a cheer in his stony heart that he now unloaded the van and stacked the contents neatly in the barn.

After his meeting with Dora, Vynce had felt the need to clear his head and took a walk across the estate to see how the operation had gone the night before. It felt strange in a pleasant sort of way to be walking out in the fresh air taking in the sights, sounds and smells that assailed his senses. It had been a while since he had been in this realm and taken corporeal form and he was almost enjoying it.

He walked over to where the van was parked and spoke to one of the small figures who held a clipboard with an air of authority.

"How did it go last night?"

The diminutive figure in the white coat ticked a box on his clipboard and looked up at the tall imposing figure that stood before him and was not at all intimidated by the difference in their sizes or status.

"Worked like a charm, boss. Got in, located the goods and got out again as smooth as you like."

He pointed to one of the white coated figures.

"Jack the Lantern there took care of the security guards, while Terrence dealt with the physical barriers and thanks to the amulet you gave us all electrical equipment was disabled or jammed. So all in all it was as sweet as a nut, sir."

Vynce looked in the barn. The haul had been greater than he had thought and there was more nerve agent than he needed, but better too much than not enough. He had been sceptical when he had hired the Cornish Piskies for the job as they had a reputation for being a bit mischievous and not reacting well to criticism. In the past he had preferred to work with elves as they always seemed fastidious in their work, but over the years they had been lured by the pay and conditions offered by the jolly fellow from the north pole so were in high demand and difficult to recruit. As a result he had not much option but to hire the piskies. So far they were doing a good job and had left a favourable impression on him. He left them to finish the unloading and headed back to the manor house.

Tea tray in hand, Sally entered the conservatory, set the tray down on the table and sat in a rattan chair next to her husband Freddy, who was spending some quality time with his collection of exotic plants while at the same time trying to get over the effects of the cloudy scrumpy he had drunk at last night's celebration. Not being a regular drinker he was suffering the consequences from trying to compete with Jed the farm hand in some local traditional drinking games. He picked up the steaming mug of tea and eyed the sandwiches suspiciously.

"What is in them?"

Sally removed the top slice of the thick farmhouse bread to reveal a generous helping of ham and mustard. Relieved, Freddy picked one up and took a bite.

"Thanks. I don't want to appear fussy but you know how sensitive the plants can be." On the stand next to Freddy the leaves of a peace lily rustled softly and its flower glowed gently from white to a pale orange and an ethereal voice radiated out from somewhere deep in its foliage.

"Hi, Sally, glad to see you took our little chat to heart about eating vegetable matter in front of us."

She sipped her tea and remembered the admonishment she had received last week from the assembled plants when she had brought Freddy a cheese and tomato sandwich. It had been a genuine mistake, but the imagery still played in her mind of how the plants viewed the taking of their young from their mothers' stalks to then be cruelly sliced and eaten with cheese. Strangely though they had no problem with the wheat that had been ground into flour to make the bread!

"Morning, Spathy; yes, I remembered our conversation and did not put any plant matter in the sandwiches today although I was a bit unsure about the mustard?"

An indignant fern hiding in a shady corner joined in.

"Mustard is acceptable. It is the exploitation of our brethren such as the tomato, cucumber and lettuce who are forced to grow in overcrowded and cramped greenhouses and poly tunnels just to satisfy the human desire for a salad or a sandwich that we feel strongly about. Especially if you then have the audacity to sit there and eat them in front of us, it is a cruel and monstrous thing to do."

A murmur of approval ran around the conservatory plants.

After sipping their tea in silence for a few moments Sally put her cup down. The conversation with the conservatory plants had diverted her from the real reason she had come in there.

She turned to her husband and with a little tremble of fear in

30

her voice spoke, "I think I saw him today in a flash car heading towards High Meadow Manor."

Freddy was confused. "Sorry, I don't understand. Who did you see?"

"Your old boss, Vynce Di-Ablo."

Freddy twitched a little and his sandwich dropped to the floor.

"Vynce! Are you sure? I thought he had gone back to wherever or whatever dimension it was he came from."

"I am certain. I recognised him in the back of his car heading up to the manor. I reckon he is the new owner of the manor and if he is back I am sure it is not for the good of humanity."

Freddy sat in stunned silence and let the news sink in, his mind racing with thoughts. Why had he come back, why here and more importantly had he come here to find him? That last thought filled him with a fear and dread that numbed his body and soul.

A little while back Freddy, who at the time had been a world-leading expert in genetic manipulation, had been hired by Vynce to genetically modify apple trees to produce a fruit that was highly psychotropic in an attempt to enslave humanity with a doughnut containing a filling made from the psychotropic apples. Like most of Vynce's schemes it never really got off the ground and had been foiled on two fronts, the first was when Sally and some of her friends destroyed the orchard. The second was a poor marketing strategy – who intentionally buys apple filled doughnuts?

It was during this time that he had first met and fallen in love with Sally. She had persuaded him to turn his back on the evil scheme and the unethical use of genetic manipulation, although she did let him keep his collection of genetically enhanced conservatory plants. Vynce had taken Freddy's betrayal very badly.

Both he and Sally sat there for a moment, each one lost in their own thoughts until they were abruptly brought back into the real world by the deep and unmistakable voice of Vinnie the giant Venus fly trap, "'Scuse me, Freddy. Are you going to eat that sandwich that fell on the floor, only you know how partial I am to a bit of ham and mustard and it would be a shame for it to go to waste."

Chapter Four

A small electric car made its way cautiously down the narrow road and through the open parkland of High Meadow Manor, coming to a stop in what used to be the walled garden which back in the day had provided the manor house with most of its fruit and vegetable needs. Times however had changed and cheap, fresh vegetables could now be delivered straight to the door, growing your own had become an uneconomic proposition, so without a second thought the greenhouses were demolished and the vegetable beds tarmacked over and turned into the staff car park.

The occupant of the car checked her hair and makeup in the rear-view mirror. Satisfied all was as it should be, she got out, closed the door, then popped open the flap for the charging port and plugged in the charging connector that was on a conveniently placed post next to the parking bay. Satisfied everything was in its place, she turned and headed towards the entrance to the offices of Di-Ablo Enterprises.

The offices of Di-Ablo Enterprises were an impressive example of modern glass and steel architecture and stood on the site of the old stables and carriage house. In a small tribute to this former use, a highly polished Landau stood in the corner of the foyer. Walking confidently up to the reception desk, the occupant of the car introduced herself.

"Hi, I'm Emma, Emma Smith, a new starter with you today. The agency sent me."

Looking up from her keyboard, the receptionist acknowledged Emma's presence with a smile. "Hello, Emma, yes we have been expecting you, bear with me a moment while I sort out your security pass."

Emma felt a chill run down her spine. There was something unnerving about the receptionist. Perhaps it was the long black robe that she wore or the greenish grey tinge to her skin tone, or the deep black unblinking eyes? Perhaps, but Emma was a modern woman and didn't judge people on their appearance. No, it was the cold unemotional serpent-like smile that had unnerved her, or maybe it was first-day nerves? She returned the smile.

After a few moments tapping away on her keyboard, the receptionist looked up from her computer screen.

"We need to take your picture for the pass. Could you look into the camera for me?"

A long bony finger pointed towards an aged Victorian camera mounted on a small wooden tripod that stood upon the reception desk.

Emma complied and looked into the lens. The receptionist then put her head under the black cloth at the rear of the camera and moved the bellows back and forward. Once satisfied everything was in focus, holding a pallet of flash powder high in one hand she pushed the shutter release with the other. There was a huge flash and smoke hung momentarily in the air before gradually fading away.

"Sorry about that. Our usual camera is not working so we are using the back-up unit until the replacement arrives."

A little shocked, Emma stepped back a pace and watched as the receptionist removed the photographic plate from the back of the camera and then threw it in the bin. She then tapped at the keyboard again and a printer whirred into life. Taking the pass from the printer she then carefully put it in a transparent plastic holder, attached a lanyard and handed it to Emma. Taking it in her hand, Emma was amazed to see a high resolution colour image of herself on the pass next to her name and the Di-Ablo company logo.

"Thanks, that is a good likeness. Normally they make you look like a crime scene picture of a gangland boss that has been found dead in the boot of a car parked in the long term parking area of an airport."

This attempt at humour fell flat.

"If you would like to take a seat someone will be with you shortly."

After a short while a door opened and a small thin man carrying an old fashioned candle lantern made his way to where Emma was sitting. "Ms Smith?"

"Hi, yes, that's me."

"Good, now if you would like to come with me I will take you to Mr Di-Ablo's office."

She looked into his old, wizened face and had the overwhelming urge follow him.

Scrolling through the contacts list on her mobile phone Sally found the one she was looking for and typed the number into the landline phone the old fashioned way. Since the fire at the mobile phone mast it was the only way she could make telephone calls from the farm without standing on a chair in the middle of the stable yard. It was a bit retro but it worked. Another alternative had been to use the phone box in the village, but due to lack of use over recent years it now housed a defibrillator. Not that the village didn't need a defibrillator, it did. Since its installation more than one heart had been restarted after sampling the delights of the signature dish from the village pub of fish and chips deep fried in goose fat washed down with a selection from their range of local ciders. The call connected and she was put through to the automated menu. After listening to the menu she selected option three, and a synthetic voice came on the line.

"Hello, unfortunately all of our operators are busy at the moment. If you leave your name and number we will call you back as soon as possible."

"Hi, this is Sally Brown from Rose Well Farm, could you call me back urgently. It is about Vynce Di-Ablo – I think he is back!"

After a short walk down a corridor and up two flights of stairs, Emma found herself outside the office door of Vynce Di-Ablo. The small man knocked on the door, and after an interval of intimidating silence a voice on the other side replied.

"Come in."

The small man opened the door and Emma walked in, the door closing behind her.

"Ah yes, you must be Emma – my new PA. They said you would be starting today." She walked up to the desk and shook the outstretched hand, it felt icily cold.

"It is good to meet you, Mr Di-Ablo, and I very much look forward to working here with you and your team."

Vynce looked her in the eye to try and get a look into her soul. She was young, confident, and if her CV was to be believed, a very capable individual, although there was something about her. He couldn't put his finger on it but he felt it in the handshake. Something nice, something good even. No matter, he would soon change that.

"It is good to meet you too, you were highly recommended

by the agency. Please take a seat."

She sat in the chair that was across the desk from him and looked around the room. It was a large modern office with the latest style of furnishings. On one side of the room stood a large conference table of a polished tubular chrome design with a deep black glass top, chairs of a similar polished chrome design sat around the table. On the wall facing the desk was a large flat screen display that showed the latest market information from around the world. It was just how she would expect the office of a modern executive to look, although one thing bothered her. On his large desk she could see a computer keyboard and monitor and she could see that information was being displayed on the screen, but there were no cables connecting the screen to a computer or even a power supply. Perhaps it was a new state-of-the-art set up she had not come across before?

Vynce reached into his desk drawer and pulled out some papers and pushed them across the table.

"Unfortunately there is the usual paperwork to take care of before we can start. Ignore the clause about taking your first born child; we don't do that anymore on advice from our legal department. Although you might want to consider the option to sell your soul as that does come with some added benefits."

Emma looked through the papers, and apart from the sections already mentioned the rest was just the usual terms and conditions and non-disclosure agreements common in most businesses, so she placed her signature and date in the required boxes, but left the option to sell her soul open.

He took the signed papers and put them in a file. He was disappointed that the soul selling option had not been taken up but there was still time.

"Splendid, that's the formalities taken care of. Before I show you where your office is and introduce you to the staff I need to tell you about fire drills, where the emergency exits and toilets are, etc. For convenience we have put this all on the company's intranet site and we have an app you can download so you can read it at your leisure."

Chapter Five

Behind the counter of the village's only pub, the Dog and Duck, the manager, Dave, was getting ready for another busy day satisfying the local need for alcohol. He prided himself that it was a friendly place where the villagers could come together and strengthen their community bonds while downing a glass or two, or even avail themselves of some good honest pub grub – the fish and chips deep fried in goose fat seemed a particular favourite and had gathered some local fame and notoriety.

He had finished polishing the glasses and was stacking them on the shelf above the bar when the door opened and a well-dressed man walked in carrying a briefcase.

"I'm afraid we're closed. If you care to come back later I will be happy to serve you then. The times are on the door."

The well-dressed man fished out a business card from the inside pocket of his jacket and continued to walk up to the bar.

"Excuse me, is the manager available?"

Dave eyed the stranger suspiciously. He was wearing a very smart and expensive looking suit and carrying a briefcase in one hand, which was at odds with his usual clientele who were as a rule normally dressed a bit more casually and had a slight whiff of the farmyard about them, apart from on a Sunday when they were dressed in their finest and smelt more of moth balls. His first guess was this could be a visit from the revenue man.

"I'm the manager. Can I help you?"

The stranger offered his card. Dave took it.

"Allow me to introduce myself. My name is Seth and I represent Di-Ablo Enterprises, I have come here to offer you the chance to become the flagship purveyor of our latest premium cider produced right here in the village up at High Meadow Manor."

Relieved that the stranger was not from the revenue, Dave relaxed a little and stopped what he was doing and looked at the card and then back at the man. His customers were quite set in their ways and tended not to stray from their favourite tipple unless there was a special offer on, besides he would have to make room for it behind his already crowded bar.

"That is a very kind offer, but we are a small village pub with an unsophisticated customer base that is reluctant to try anything new so I am not sure we would be the best pub to become your flagship. You might be better trying the Pickled Parsnip over in Thriphampton; they tend to get a more diverse patronage being as they are closer to the town."

Undeterred, Seth placed his briefcase on the bar, flipped the catches and opened the lid. "That is unfortunate. We selected you as our first choice as we the manufacturer are right here in the same village so we could do each other some good. Mr Di-Ablo values his privacy and is not keen to have a shop at the manor, so he thought the village pub would be the ideal place to not only offer this premium cider to its customers but also handle any local retail sales and of course there would be a favourable discount."

Dave scratched his chin. The thought of retail sales appealed to him especially if it increased footfall through his pub, but on the other hand he didn't want to be stuck with stock he could not sell.

"It is a tempting offer but I am not sure it is for us."

Sensing indecision, Seth took his opportunity and removed

a small sample bottle from his briefcase.

"Perhaps you would like try some to help you make up your mind."

Pouring a small amount into a glass, the bar manager held it up to the light to check the clarity, then gave it a tentative sniff before taking a sip. As he sipped the golden brew he felt the flavour explode on his tongue, then suddenly without warning every nerve in his body seemed to tingle as the liquid nectar made its way down his throat and into his stomach. It was the best drink he had ever tasted, strangely satisfying but extremely moreish.

"Yes, it is nice, very nice indeed. Now, you mentioned a discount earlier, what sort of figure are we looking at?"

After briefing Emma on the company's latest enterprise, the manufacture of a premium cider, Vynce then introduced her to the office staff and took her on a tour of the manufacturing facility to show her how the product was made and introduce her to the manufacturing team. It was her first time in a brewery and the warm, sweet alcohol laden air was like nothing she had experienced before and made her feel a little light headed.

Vynce pointed to one of the large stainless steel fermenting vessels.

"The juice from the apple press is routed through those pipes and into these fermentation bins where we add a little yeast to get things going and then heat it to turn all of those natural sugars into alcohol. To make sure we produce a consistent quality product each step of the process is strictly monitored and controlled by our team of master brewers."

Moving her gaze in the direction of Vynce's pointing she noticed a group of small men in white coats, respirators, and chemical proof gloves pouring the contents of a two hundred litre drum into the fermenting vessel.

Suddenly interested in the process she asked, "What are they doing? Is that some sort of chemical additive?"

Vynce stepped between her and the activity of the white-coated men in an effort to block her view.

"Oh that. No, it's not a chemical as such, more of an ingredient, just an acidity regulator we put in to make sure we have a consistent product."

Emma was not convinced.

"Didn't the drum have a biohazard sign on it and the men did seem to be wearing protective equipment!"

"No, I am sure it didn't, probably just a manufacturer's logo and, well, you know what health and safety are like about protective equipment. Now come this way and I will show you the bottling plant."

Picking up the phone he could hear silence on the other end. Thinking that it was another scam call to inform him that his internet connection was causing chaos in the world of cyber communications, he was just about to say something uncharitable and hang up when there was a loud click on the line and a soft female voice spoke.

"Hello, Freddy, we received the message from your wife. We were aware of the return of Mr Di-Ablo but it is good to have an independent report of his reappearance."

Freddy felt the strength drain from his knees and he had to sit down. The voice continued and Freddy listened and as he listened he could feel panic filling the very fibre of his being. After the call he quickly put the phone down and rushed off to find Sally.

He found her out in the paddock grooming Flotsam and

Jetsam, her prize winning pet ponies. Watching as he rushed across the paddock towards her, she stopped what she was doing. Despite his exertion his face was a deathly grey.

"What's up? Has Ted put his fingers in the tractor charging socket again?"

Freddy gulped down some air. "It's worse than that, they have just called back. You were right, Vyncent Di-Ablo is back, right here in the village at High Meadow Manor."

Sally stood motionless for a moment as the news sank in.

"Did they say why he was back? Does he know we are here?"

"They are not sure why he has suddenly turned up here and they don't seem to think he is aware of our presence. They have sent an operative to the area to try and find out what he is up to, but they are pretty sure he is setting up another one of his plots to try and subvert the will of humanity."

Sally did not like what she was hearing. They had helped the organisation before in its fight against the forces of darkness, it had been a close fought battle and she had no desire for a re-match.

"If they are sending an operative to investigate I guess we can sit on the side lines and let the two sides slug it out."

Freddy looked at his feet to try and avoid Sally's gaze.

"Not quite. They have asked us to, if necessary, be a go between, between them and their operative. You know, getting messages back and forth, that sort of thing. They will let us know if and when they need our help."

She shook her head. She had no desire to get involved, but if it was just a matter of getting messages back and forth she could see no harm in that. Seeing that Flotsam and Jetsam had become disinterested and wandered off to nibble on a patch of clover, she picked up her kit and started to head back to the farm house.

"Come on, Freddy, after a shock like that I need a cup of tea and maybe a biscuit." At the sound of the word biscuit Freddy's mood lightened slightly.

"Biscuits, I thought you said we had run out!"

After the site tour Emma had settled down in her office and started to get herself organised. Vynce had given her a list of tasks to do. There was a big meeting tomorrow between Vynce and the stakeholders in his new business venture and she was busy sorting out agendas and organising sample packs and a myriad of other things to make sure the meeting went smoothly. Going through the list of attendees, there were some names she vaguely recognised but couldn't say where or why they seemed familiar. Taking her phone out of her bag she checked the signal strength, there was no coverage. That was a nuisance, her first thought had been to use the camera and livestream the image back to base for them to analyse, leaving very little in the way of evidence on her phone. Instead she would now have to photograph the list and hide the image in an obscure file in an attempt to try and outwit security in the event they wanted to look through her phone as she entered and left the building. She took the pictures and hoped for the best.

Much to their dismay the call had come through late in the afternoon, they were to go to the Dog and Duck that evening where they would make contact with the operative who would then give them a package. Further instructions on what to do with the package would follow. So it was with much reluctance that Freddy and Sally strolled down the lane towards the village pub.

It was a pleasant autumnal evening. The sun had just gone down and the air was starting to chill. There were no streetlights in the lane and both were a little edgy as they walked through the darkness jumping slightly every time the breeze rustled the leaves or when the animals moved about in the fields.

In contrast, the lounge of the Dog and Duck was warm and cosy as they made their way to the bar.

Dave greeted them in his usual genial way, "Good evening, Freddy, Sally, what can I get you?"

Freddy had been given strict instructions by Sally that they needed to have their wits about them this evening and so they should not dull them with alcohol. Reluctantly he had agreed, although he was sure a stiff whiskey would have helped ease the nerves.

"Hi, Dave, two orange juices please."

"Would you like ice with them?"

Freddy gave his assent and looked around room, at first glance there was no one he did not recognise and he turned his attention back to the barman who was busy pouring orange juice into two glasses. As he watched the glasses fill he became aware of a young smartly dressed woman standing beside him. She had not been there a moment ago and he had not heard her walk up to the bar. Dave looked up and acknowledged her.

"Hi, Emma, if you care to take a seat I will get them to bring your meal over to you in a moment."

She thanked the barman, then turned and smiled at Freddy and with practised ease dropped an SD card unnoticed into one of the glasses of orange juice and walked over to an empty table.

Freddy tapped his debit card on the card reader and picked up his drinks and was just about to head off to the table by the window where Sally was now seated when curiosity got the better of him.

"Who was that young lady that was standing here a moment ago? I didn't recognise her, mind you, I don't get away from the farm that often these days."

"Oh that was Emma, she is lodging with us for a while, she has just started a new job up at the manor. I think she is the PA to the big boss or something like that."

They had been sat there for quite a while and nothing out of the ordinary had happened so far. No shadowy figures with hats pulled down and collars pulled up to obscure their faces had approached them to hand them a brown paper envelope. Instead it had just been another evening in the village pub, there was a buzz of conversation with the occasional bit of laughter thrown in, Ted and Jed were unwinding after a hard day's work on the farm with a couple of pints and a game of darts while a log burnt lazily on the open fire.

Freddy leaned over the table and whispered, "That must be her over there eating her dinner. I am sure of it."

"Maybe, but she has not shown any sign that she wants to contact us. Oh, hold on, she is standing up."

They both tried to appear nonchalant as Emma stood up, retrieved her room key from the table and walked away towards the door. Disappointed that he had been wrong, Freddy looked at his almost empty glass.

"Well, it can't be her then. I guess we will just have to wait a little longer. Do you fancy another?"

So saying he drained the remaining orange juice into his mouth where the SD card lodged in the back of his throat making him gag a little. He gave a cough and the SD card released its grip and landed in his open palm.

"It must have been Dave. I mean who else would have had a

chance to slip it in my drink? I could have choked on that; I am going to have a word next time I see him."

Sally was unconvinced.

"I am not so sure. They said they were sending an operative not that there was one already embedded in the village, it must be someone else! Did you bump into anyone when you brought the drinks over to the table?"

"No. I did not get near enough to anyone for them to spike our drinks with electronic memory cards. Let's take it and get out before Dave starts to serve silicon chips with his fried fish!"

Walking back to the farm and mulling the evening's events over in his mind, Freddy was just about to speak when he heard the sound of a car approaching from behind. As there was no footpath in the lane they both instinctively stopped and stood to one side to let the car pass. Instead of passing them the car slowed down and stopped right by where they stood. In the darkness they could just make out the shape of an old Morris Minor car, the driver wound down their window.

"Hello, sorry to bother you but I am looking for Rose Well Farm. Do you know if I am on the right road, only the sat nav is playing up a bit?"

Stooping slightly, Freddy tried to get a better look at the driver. He had a vague idea who might be driving a Morris Minor around the lanes this time of night. He was not disappointed as he saw the face of a woman wearing a nun's habit looking back at him. "Yes, it is just down the lane on the left. We are going that way if you could give us a lift."

The nun took the smart phone from off its cradle on the dashboard, put the camera in front of Freddy's face and tapped the screen. The facial recognition software confirmed who he was; she then did the same for Sally. Satisfied they were who she thought they might be, she put the phone back in its cradle.

"Freddy, Sally, it is nice to meet you, Sister Susan sends her regards. Now I believe you have something for me?"

Chapter Six

Around the large conference table sat Vynce's inner circle. They all came from the higher echelons of society and many were well known figures from around the county: among them were the local MP, the county's police chief, various members of the local council and some business leaders. Most would call themselves friends of Vynce Di-Ablo but one or two could be considered rivals. He did not mind that some of his rivals were part of his inner circle, in fact, he preferred it this way. Not only did it give them a false sense of security, it also meant he could keep his eye on them. In the event of problems they would be used as scapegoats and sacrificed for the greater good of the rest of the group. Sitting at the head of the table he called the meeting to order.

"Ladies and gentlemen, thank you all for coming, it is really good to see you all again. Now if I may, let's get down to business. Do you all have a copy of the agenda?"

Heads nodded and a ripple of approval ran around the table.

"Good. Now as you are all aware the plan for me to take over the world and become its new emperor and incidentally make you all very rich and powerful along the way is progressing on schedule. As you can see from your briefing pack we have procured the necessary nerve agent and have successfully combined it with fermented apple juice to produce a highly addictive and psychotropic cider. Once imbibed by an unsuspecting public it will make them susceptible to our subliminal programming, supressing any resistance there may be to our goal of world domination."

A hand went up.

"Can I ask a question?"

Vynce stopped his presentation. The hand belonged to a local councillor, who only held the position because he came from an influential family. He was one of Vynce's scapegoats. "Of course, I am happy to explain any aspects of the plan that you may be unsure about."

"Thank you, Mister Di-Ablo, I am a little worried about the use of the nerve agent on the general population. It sounds a little dangerous to me. Are we sure it is safe?"

Vynce moved his head in the direction of the person sat to his right. "That is a good question. It is a complex technical matter that is probably better explained by my master brewer, Jasmine."

Jasmine stood up and connected her tablet through the secure wi-fi connection to a projector that hung from the ceiling. She was an ambitious woman in her late twenties, who had once been on track to gain a PhD in chemistry until she found she had a talent for making illicit substances and exploiting the needs of her fellow students. A talent that was cut short one night after a small explosion and fire damaged the chemistry lab and exposed her scheme.

She poked at the screen on her tablet and a complex looking equation was projected onto the far wall.

Emma, who had been sitting quietly away from the main group taking the meeting minutes, got up, closed the blinds and switched off the lights.

During her presentation, Jasmine ran through the various aspects of the fermentation process, explaining in detail the chemical processes that occurred at different stages of the procedure and identified the key time window of when to add the nerve agent.

"So as you can see, if the nerve agent is added during this window here the fermenting apple juice will break down some of its bonds and convert it from a lethal poison into a sweet tasting highly addictive psychotropic liquid that can be used for behavioural modification. I hope this has explained the process – any questions?"

The room was silent. Most of those sat around the table had no idea or understanding of what had just been said, it had gone way over their heads.

Vynce looked at the local councillor. "Does that answer your question?"

The councillor shifted uneasily in his chair and fiddled with his tie. He had not understood any of the slides or the explanations from the presentation but he had a position to uphold and did not want to appear foolish in front of everybody so he nodded his head in agreement.

Vynce surveyed the blank expressions on the faces around the table. He was losing them; a different approach was required.

"I don't know about you but that was a lot of information to take in. Jasmine could you put up the other slide with the simplified explanation."

Jasmine poked at the tablet's touch screen and a new slide was displayed. It was a simple graphic that showed a picture of an apple, a plus sign and a drum with a biohazard sign on it. To the right of this there was an equal's sign followed by an image of the earth with a wheel clamp on it, a smiley face, and a pound sign wearing a top hat and smoking a cigar. On seeing this new slide a wave of approval ran around the table followed by loud cheering and a round of applause.

As the applause died down, Vynce tapped the keys on his laptop and a promotional picture of the finished bottled product projected itself onto the far wall.

"Here is a picture of the finished product that we will be using in our advertising campaign. As you can see we have had to change the product name as the marketing department thought that the original name of 'Badger's Armpit' might not go down too well with the more modern, sophisticated cliental that we are aiming for, so we have renamed it 'Di-Ablo's Revenge' which I hope you will agree is a more fitting name that reflects its true purpose." Vynce tapped his keyboard again and a picture of the village pub replaced the promotional picture. "You will all be pleased to know that our local village pub the 'Dog and Duck' has signed up to be the first outlet for our merchandise and will be the perfect testing ground to iron out any bugs in the product before we go nationwide and indeed worldwide. Gentlemen, welcome to the new world order."

A round of applause once again ran around the table.

Checking that he was not standing in any puddles and that his rubber gloves were on properly, Ted unplugged the electric tractor from the charging point and admonished Jed, the farm labourer who had been washing the day's muck off the electric work horse with a hose. "I don't think it is wise to do that while it is plugged in."

Unfazed, Jed carried on.

"You worry too much. Remember that rep that came down here to demonstrate it. I distinctly remember him saying that is was completely watertight even when charging after you asked him if it was safe to use in the rain."

Ted stroked the stubble on his chin. He remembered the rep, a slippery character who knew very little about farming but proceeded tell Ted how he should go about running things, not a man he could readily trust, but on this occasion Ted grudgingly conceded he might be right.

"Well. All right then but be careful and remember to plug it in again, we need to plough ten acre field tomorrow and I don't want a repeat of last time when you ran out of battery and I had to get Jethro and his shire horse Hercules to tow you back here. I am still buying him a pint every time I see him down the Dog and Duck to keep it quiet."

Jed focused a jet of water on some stubborn organic matter that was sticking to the tread of the tyres and smiled inwardly at the incident and the irony of the latest in farming technology being recovered by some of the oldest. Technology in his opinion was all well and good but sometimes you could not beat the old ways, although to be fair to the tractor, as it was charged by power harvested by the farm's own solar panels it probably created less in the way of greenhouse gasses than Hercules.

"Right you are. Now you mention the Dog and Duck, will you be down there this evening? They are having a bit of a do apparently, launching a new brand of cider brewed up there at the manor. They are even laying on some sort of buffet."

Ted thought for a moment, he was tempted by the offer, it would be nice to wind down after a hard day's work with a cider and a mini pork pie, but he was a little set in his ways and knew what he liked. He had no desire to change his drink of choice and would stick with his normal poison. This newcomer would just have to wait a little longer so he made his excuses.

"Not tonight, Jed, I promised the missus I would make a start on wallpapering the back bedroom ready for when her sister comes to stay."

Emma busied herself tidying up the coffee cups and other bits of detritus left over from the meeting. Vynce had taken his guests on a personal guided tour of the production facility in an attempt to keep them on-board and allay any lingering doubts as to how and where their money was being spent. Each of them had invested a considerable sum in this venture on the promise of an incredibly large return and a position of authority in the new world order that would come with Vynce's rise to power as emperor of the world. She put the coffee cups in the dishwasher and headed back to her office to type up the minutes.

Sitting at her desk, she tapped away at the keyboard, troubled by what she had seen and heard during the meeting. When she had been briefed about the assignment she was aware that this was a high profile mission, but she was beginning to think that even her superiors in the organisation had underestimated what was going on here.

It was true she had been sent by an agency to fill the role of PA to Vyncent Di-Ablo. But the agency in question was not your average employment agency that hired out office staff on a contract basis. It was in fact an ancient, secret society set up by the world's major religions in order to combat the threats posed by the dark forces of evil that tried every so often to take control of the world and corrupt the path of humanity, and it was this agency that had sent her to spy on him. Vynce had been on the society's radar for many centuries, popping up at various stages of humanity's evolution with a usually half-baked scheme to bend the will of humanity to his evil ways. Most of his plots were harmless and had little effect on humanity's advancement. He was not one of the underworld's greatest demons but he was persistent, and this time things were looking a little more serious.

If what she had read in the briefing notes were true, his last plot to enslave humanity with psychotropic doughnuts was only foiled by the bravery and determination of one of her colleagues who along with some civilian help and an error in his marketing strategy of using an apple filling instead of raspberry in the doughnuts brought the scheme to an end. This time though, it looked like he had the marketing strategy right and was on course to make his mind-bending cider a huge success.

Just as she was emailing the meeting minutes to the attendees, there was a knock on the door and a small, wizened man entered the office pushing a trolley containing the post. She waved him into the office. "Hi, Pomery. Is that the post for Mr Di-Ablo?"

Pomery nodded and placed the bundle of post and a small parcel on her desk. From her training she had recognised that the myriad of small people that seemed to make up the majority of the work force at Di-Ablo Enterprises were Cornish Piskies. This was not in itself strange as many of the underworld's key players preferred a non-human workforce; they were more loyal and asked less questions than the average human so tended to get on with things with the minimum of fuss. The only question was why piskies? Due to their slightly better work ethic elves were normally considered the go-to guys if you wanted a job done. She brushed the question aside; it was one for the analysts back at head office to answer.

As Pomery wheeled his trolley out of the office she scanned through the mail, filtered out the junk and took it through to Vynce's office. He was still out on his site tour. Lifting the small parcel her attention was drawn by its weight, for its size it seemed very heavy. She looked at the label, and it read, "To be opened by addressee only." She put it on his desk and made a mental note to try and find out what it might be.

Chapter Seven

It was late evening, Vynce sat at his desk in his office in darkness, a faint glow of light seeped in from the emergency light in the corridor through the gap between the frame and the ill-fitting door. Sitting opposite him wearing her blackest of robes was Mother Evandoria, leader of the local witches' coven. Between them sat the contents of the parcel that had been delivered to his office earlier that day.

"Thank you for coming, Dora. I am a little out of practice with this and appreciate your help."

Dora nodded. She felt a little tinge of pride that she was now sat in front of one of the underworld's premier demons giving him a refresher course in the art of crystal ball reading. She usually preferred to do her readings in the stuffy atmosphere of her back room that she had meticulously furnished in the style preferred by mediums of the Victorian era. This she thought gave the right ambience and met with the expectations of the paying punters. If the truth were told she felt a little out of place in the modern surroundings of Vynce's office, but after all she was a professional and would give it her best shot whatever the setting.

"Thank you, Vynce, it is an honour. Now what was it you wanted to see?"

She took three deep breaths and then waved her hands slowly over the crystal ball, concentrating hard on the subject Vynce had described. A mist appeared in the fabric of the crystal ball. It grew steadily thicker before gradually starting to recede, revealing a fuzzy image. The image was a low definition picture of a crowd of people that kept fading in and out of the haze. Concentrating hard, Vynce looked at the familiar faces in the crowd. It was a crowd containing the same people that had sat around his meeting table earlier in the day, each individual was in a different place, some were at home, and some were in other people's homes, while others were journeying back to their families. Through the purity and the natural resonance frequency of the crystal sphere, Vynce and Dora had managed to focus the life forces of all the individuals into one small area contained within the ball. He concentrated harder and could hear their voices, then as he focused he gradually became able to tune into the thoughts in their heads. He sifted through these thoughts, discarding the mundane, such as what they would like for dinner or how their new shoes were causing their bunions to play up again, until he located the ones related to his plan.

One by one he probed their inner most thoughts until he was satisfied he had the information he needed. Most were committed to the plan and were loyal to him and his ambitions, but he had found one lone stray thought that was less than pure to the cause. He made a mental note to keep an eye on that potential troublemaker.

In the Dog and Duck the evening was going with a swing. Behind the bar Dave was struggling to keep up with the demand for the new cider and the buffet had been all but demolished. Of those that had tried Di-Ablo's Revenge, most agreed it was the best drink that they had ever drunk and were eager for more.

In a corner under a promotional banner that read "Try Di-Ablo's Revenge. It's devilishly good" sat Seth the sales rep for Di-Ablo Enterprises. From what he could see sales were exceeding expectations and it appeared people were becoming hooked as predicted; he had a lot of good news to report back to the boss.

Sat at another table finishing the last forkful of the house speciality of fish and chips deep fried in goose fat and drinking a glass of mineral water was Emma. She was also taking mental notes and although not showing it she was alarmed at what she was witnessing. The new product was being consumed at an astonishing rate and as expected people were becoming quite merry, but the strange thing was that from her observations no matter how much an individual drank they never seemed to get any drunker. Once they reached the 'merry' stage that's where they stayed. By her reckoning at least two of the revellers should be passed out stone cold on the floor by now.

Getting up from her chair, she noticed Seth sitting in the corner nursing his orange juice and occasionally writing in his notebook. She had been introduced to him during her guided tour of the plant and had taken an instant dislike to him. In her limited experience all sales reps were a little slippery and not to be trusted, but from her short conversation with him he seemed greasier than most. She made her way over to where he was sitting.

"Hi. It's Seth, isn't it? I'm Emma Vynce's new PA. We met the other day back in the office." Seth stopped scribbling in his book and looked up. As he looked up she could feel his cold heartless eyes scanning her body and she felt a little uneasy. He held out his hand in greeting.

"Ah yes, Seth, that's me. Just making sure the launch of the new cider gets off to a good start."

"Judging by what I have seen it seems to be a big hit. I am sure Vynce will be pleased."

"I am sure he will. It seems to be going better than expected.

Once we are established here we can start to focus on national and then international sales – the world's our oyster. Can I get you one, on the firm, of course?"

There were many reasons that Emma did not want to sample the product or spend any more time than was necessary in Seth's company, but she remained polite.

"That's kind of you, Seth, but I have a full day tomorrow and just want to get away and clear my head for a bit, maybe some other time?"

Sally sat on the bench next to the war memorial on the village green as she had been instructed to do by the occupant of the Morris Minor they had met the other night. In her hand she held the mobile phone she had been given. She looked at the time displayed on the screen, she was in the right place at the right time, but there was no sign of her contact. As she sat there wondering what to do, her phone vibrated and she became aware of a young smartly dressed businesswoman sitting down on the bench next to her. The woman smiled at Sally, fished around in her bag, pulled out her phone and swiped at the screen.

Looking disappointed, the woman turned to Sally. "Oh dear, I can't seem to get a signal."

"No, unfortunately since the mobile mast burned down there has been no coverage in the village. You may need to drive further down the road to get a good connection."

Emma put her phone back in her bag and stood up.

"That is a nuisance. I am expecting an important call."

As Emma walked away Sally felt her phone vibrate again and the message 'Download complete' flashed up on the screen.

Back in the safety of her own kitchen Sally put the kettle on, sat at the kitchen table and looked at the phone's screen. The previous download message had gone and had been replaced with the default screensaver picture and the time and date.

"How did it go? Did you meet the mysterious agent?"

Freddy had heard her come in and was now in the kitchen pouring boiling water over some organic tea bags.

"Um, yes, well I think so. I was sat on the bench by the war memorial like we were told to when a smartly dressed woman sat down next to me. When she realised there was no mobile signal she got up again and left. That's when the phone told me the download was complete."

Freddy sipped his tea and listened to the story. It did seem a little odd, maybe he had watched too many old spy thrillers but they had expected to have been contacted by a man in a raincoat with his collar pulled up, wearing a hat and dark glasses to obscure his face from prying eyes, he would then have placed a folded up newspaper containing the secret file on the bench before making his excuses and walking away, leaving the newspaper and its clandestine contents to be casually picked up by Sally. It seemed like reality was different from the movies.

"Did you get a look at her?"

Sally nodded.

"I am sure it was the lady we saw the other night at the Dog and Duck. The one that Dave said was Vynce's new PA. It happened so quickly but I am sure it was her."

As they sat around the table drinking tea the phone buzzed and bleeped. Sally picked it up and listened to the voice on the other end.

In the cab of the tractor Jed sat in silence listening to the birds that were calling out to each other from the trees and hedgerows that bordered ten acre field. As he sat there he thought how lucky he was to be working in such a calm and pleasing environment and to have ten acre field and the surrounding countryside as the view from his office window. It was true he could probably earn more money working in an office or a factory, but money wasn't everything and deep down he knew he would feel trapped working anywhere else but outdoors. Not that he was poorly paid; Freddy and Sally were more than generous compared with some of the other farmers around the village, and besides, working on the farm helping to keep the nation fed was good, honest, important work.

Looking out towards the entrance of the field Jed could see Ted, Jethro and Hercules making their way over to where he was stuck in the middle of the field with a flat battery. He got down from the cab and enjoyed the last few moments of calm before Ted got within earshot.

While Jethro was busy connecting Hercules's harness to a sturdy mounting point on the front of the tractor an exasperated Ted was bending Jed's ear.

"This is the second time this has happened now! I told you to make sure it was fully charged before you started out."

"Sorry, Jed. It slipped my mind to plug it in again after I cleaned it. Besides it was you that unplugged it yesterday."

"That's as may be, but be more careful in future, the weather is due to turn in a day or two and we need it ploughed before then otherwise we will be behind schedule."

Jed nodded in acceptance of his rebuke from the farm manager.

Seeing that his point had been made, Ted could feel his frustration ebb a little and he patted his workmate on the shoulder.

"It's your turn to get the beers in for Jethro's help, and I promised Hercules a bag of oats for his troubles too."

After checking all was secure, Jethro gave the thumbs up to Jed who was now back in the cab of the lifeless tractor, Jed acknowledged the signal, and with a command from Jethro, Hercules took the strain and plodded his way across the field with the tractor in tow and for a second time hauled it back to Rose Well Farm.

Pomery was not his usual chirpy self as he went about his business. Unlike demons such as Vynce Di-Ablo, the Cornish Piskie has a normally cheerful if often mischievous demeanour, but today his usual carefree happy manner had been replaced by a more subdued one.

Gone was his normal cheery banter with the other staff as he pushed his post trolley through the open plan offices delivering the mail and other internal documents. Instead he wheeled his trolley in silence while he tried to straighten out the thoughts that were tumbling around inside his head. He was troubled. The source of the trouble was the new female human that was working as Vynce's PA.

Piskies are creatures that enjoy the outdoor life and do not like being cooped up inside for long periods, so since starting to work at Di-Ablo Enterprises Pomery had got into the habit of taking a walk around the grounds of High Meadow Manor to enjoy the splendour of the natural world before starting his confining office duties. This morning he had a bit more time than usual and had wandered a little further afield and as such found himself at the hedge that bordered the village green. It was here he had seen the troubling sight. Being inquisitive, he had peeked through the hedge to see what the humans were up to and had seen Emma the new PA sit on the seat next to another human female that he did not recognise and speak to her. From his understanding of humans this was a normal social interaction and did not trouble him, but it was what had happened next that was the source of his anxiety. As Emma had sat down he was aware of a strange high frequency buzzing, inaudible to humans but within the frequency range of his highly sensitive ears. Having sensitive ears was one of the reasons piskies had in recent times reduced their contact with humans and had retreated to some of the more remote and desolate areas of Cornwall. This had been in an effort to get away from the pollution caused by the high frequency electromagnetic waves that humans had come to use as their favoured method of long distance communication. Although not involved, he and his colleagues had been pleased when the phone mast had been destroyed and they enjoyed the respite it gave them from the human pollution of the electromagnetic spectrum.

In this case he recognised the buzzing as the passing of data between the mobile communication devices that humans were so fond of. This troubled him greatly. Was Emma in secret communication with this other human, or was it just the normal interactions between the mobile devices?

He felt conflicted, should he report his suspicions to Vynce or just chalk it up as one of those coincidences? If he was right and Emma was leaking information, Vynce would be very pleased and life could become a whole lot better for him, but if he was wrong, Vynce was known for not suffering fools gladly and things could get unpleasant for him very quickly. It was with these contradictory thoughts whirling about in his head he went about his duties. After much thought and deliberation throughout the day he came to the conclusion that perhaps this was something he should discuss with his colleagues first before speaking with Vynce.

Chapter Eight

Things were going well at Di-Ablo Enterprises and despite his normal demonic disposition to being irritable, Vynce was in a good mood. Seth had just left after briefing him on the launch of 'Di-Ablo's Revenge'. Looking at the night's sales figures they had exceeded expectations by a fair margin. Leaning back in his chair, he allowed himself a small malevolent cackle before contemplating his next move.

According to the plan the next move was to check that those who had partaken of the evil brew could be manipulated into doing his bidding. He took the crystal ball from his desk, closed the blinds and buzzed Emma on the intercom to tell her he was not to be disturbed. Taking deep breaths and waving his hands over the crystal ball in the same way as he had seen Dora do the other evening, he looked deep into the recesses of the crystal, and the mist cleared to show the village centre and the villagers going about their mundane daily lives. Smiling inwardly, he thought he had just the thing that would test the effectiveness of the mind controlling cider. Waving his arms once more and muttering a sacred incantation, he watched as the mist descended again in the crystal sphere before slowly clearing to show a new image of the village.

Ted had asked Jethro to take Hercules on a circuitous route back to the farm avoiding the village centre and any embarrassment that this may have caused. But despite his best efforts, Jethro had not been able to stop Hercules from taking the direct route through the village. Hercules for his part was enjoying pulling the tractor and intended to show as many humans as possible that while modern machinery may be all well and good, they would be well warned not to turn their backs on some of the traditional, more organic methods.

As they approached the village, a smug-feeling Hercules sensed an unnatural presence and slowed to a stop. Ted and Jethro, who had been walking alongside him, also stopped and despite their best efforts could not get him to move; the more they coaxed him the more he dug his hooves in.

Climbing down from his cab, Jed was about to join his colleagues to see what the holdup was when he was amazed to see a number of the villagers coming out of their houses in a trance-like state and head towards the village green. Once assembled, the crowd then started to perform an impromptu Morris dance. The three men and the horse stood in astonished silence and watched the spectacle unfold before them. Then as suddenly as it had begun the crowd stopped dancing, dispersed and headed back to their homes as if nothing unusual had happened. Jethro scratched the stubble on his chin and looked at Ted.

"Old Harry ain't going to like that, you know how possessive he is about the Morris dancing team and the practice schedules."

Unimpressed, Hercules snorted and started off again towards the farm.

Vynce sat back in his chair and allowed himself another small cackle. He was pleased with the results he had witnessed in the crystal ball. If he could get them to Morris dance on the village green he would certainly be able to get the humans to do anything.

He was just about to pick up the crystal ball and put it back in his desk draw when his attention was drawn to what at first he thought was an imperfection in the crystal. It wasn't unusual to see tiny flaws in some of the cheaper, lower-end crystal balls, but this one was a high quality crystal that had been handed down through the generations and had a good proven track record. He looked more closely at the flaw, concentrating his mind on the small red fleck deep within the crystal, and the harder he concentrated the larger the image grew until he could see an image of a smartly dressed human female sitting at a computer. The figure was pulling up documents on the computer screen and photographing them with the camera on her phone. The image was fuzzy so he could not make out their face, but he recognised the office. It was the one next to his, the office of Emma, his PA.

He sat back in his chair to consider the implications of this vision and cursed himself for not spotting it earlier. All the signs were there right from the start, the feeling of goodness he had felt at their first meeting and the refusal to take up the offer of selling her soul and all of its attendant benefits. How could he have missed it? She was an agent sent by the 'other side', the forces of good that watch over humanity protecting them from the universe's darker elements, such as himself. The question was how much had she managed to report back and what to do about it?

In her office Emma felt a chill run down her spine. She switched off the camera on her phone and put the phone in her bag. Her training had taught her a technique to enable her to tune into some of the subconscious thoughts in her mind, isolate and analyse them. As one of her instructors at the academy had once told her, "If you have the feeling you are being watched, you most probably are."

In her subconscious mind she had the uneasy feeling that she had been found out and needed to get out of there quickly. She ran through the options in her conscious mind. She would get out but not so rapidly that it would arouse suspicion, it was almost lunch time. She would slip out of the office on the pretext (if anyone asked) of getting a sandwich from the village bakery, get her stuff from her room at the Dog and Duck and high-tail it back to headquarters to break the bad news personally to her bosses.

It was a slightly nervous but less troubled Pomery that made his way through the open plan office and up to the top floor to the executive suite where Vynce had his office. He had sought advice from some of the Piskie elders on what to do with the problem that had been bothering him. The consensus was that they had a duty to let Vynce know what was going on as he was their employer and boss. Not that they were being well paid for their endeavours, it was more out of a sense of loyalty and the hint from Vynce that they would have a greater role in world affairs once he had taken over.

Vynce sat at his desk, leaned forward, and looked down at the figure that stood in front of him and listened to the story that Pomery was getting off his chest. He leaned forward a bit more, not because he couldn't hear what was being said, but because he could only see the top of the head of the diminutive figure that stood before him. As he leant in he could now see the face of the Piskie standing in front of him, and he looked deep into the eyes and into the soul of the figure standing cap in hand at his desk. The Piskie was sincere in what he was saying. After Pomery had stopped talking Vynce sat back in his chair to think. In doing so he lost eye contact and could only see some wispy hair and the tips of Pomery's pointy ears.

He leant forward again, and said, "Thank you, Pomery, for bring this to my attention. It confirms something I had my suspicions about. You will be rewarded for bringing this to my attention. Leave this with me and keep it under your hat for now, I don't want it to go any further."

Pomery looked at the cap he was clutching in his slightly sweaty hands and then back at Vynce. "Thank you, sir, I won't say a word."

A thin, serpent-like smile spread across the face of Vynce Di-Ablo. "Thank you, Pomery. That will be all for now, but if you could ask Jack the Lantern to come up to me immediately, I have an urgent job for him."

Back at the farm, Hercules, with some direction from Jethro, had manoeuvred the tractor into its charging bay and Jethro was busy uncoupling the horse from the tractor.

"Are you sure you wouldn't like me and Hercules here to do a bit of that ploughing for you while your electric horse there is charging, I'm sure we could get a fair bit done in that time."

Ted took off his cloth cap and ran his hand over the top of his head. It was a tempting offer as the weather was due to turn in a day or two and it would be good to get a bit further forward. But with a full charge and a bit of luck it should be possible to get the field ploughed in time.

"Thanks for the offer, Jethro, but I think we will be able to manage."

Jethro pulled on Hercules's reigns and the two of them started to plod their way out of the yard.

"Well, if you change your mind you know where I am, and don't forget you owe me a pint or two and a bag of oats for Hercules here."

With a cheery wave the man and his shire horse plodded their way up the farm track and headed home, both with satisfied smiles on their faces.

Striding confidently across the foyer, Emma stopped at the reception desk to let the receptionist know she was popping into the village to run some errands and would not be long. Her outward projection of confidence contrasted with what she was feeling inside. Inside she was afraid that any moment she would be stopped by one of Vynce's henchmen and hauled back to his office to explain herself, or worse. Only a few more steps and she would be through the glass doors and outside of the building, then a few steps more and she would be in the carpark and the relative safety of her car. So far so good.

As she approached her car she became aware of a small figure leaning on the charging stand where her car was waiting, plugged in, battery at full capacity, and ready for a quick getaway. As she got nearer she saw that the figure was holding an old fashioned candle lantern. Her heart sank and she could feel the cold fingers of fear slowly spread through her mind and body – it was Jack the Lantern.

"Hi, Emma, would you come with me, the boss would like a word."

Mesmerised by the warm scented light emanating from the lantern, she fought the compelling urge to follow the small man and struggled desperately to press the button on her key fob and unlock the door, but as hard as she fought she could not open the car door nor could she run away. She no longer had control over her legs that were now starting to feel very heavy. Slowly she could feel the fight drain from her and in a trance-like state she complied and followed Jack away from the main building and out into the vast grounds of High Meadow Manor.

Chapter Nine

Sally was awoken from her warm comforting sleep by the sound of loud, persistent and urgent banging on the front door. She looked at the alarm clock. It was just after two in the morning, who could be calling on them at this hour of the night? She put on a robe and looked out the window and suddenly understood the urgency. Illuminated by the weak moonlight she could see parked in the stable yard an aged Morris Minor car and in the shadows she could just make out a figure dressed in a black robe banging on her door. She looked over to her husband for reassurance but Freddy was flat out on his back snoring rhythmically, totally oblivious of the noise made by their nocturnal visitor.

After double checking through the peep hole, Sally cautiously opened the door and let in the black-robed visitor.

"You will have to excuse me; it is early in the morning and my mind is still away with the fairies somewhere over in Bedfordshire. Let me get this clear in my mind so there can be no mistake. You are saying that your agent 'Emma' has gone missing and you think she may have been abducted by Vynce Di-Ablo?"

The nun nodded and sat down at the kitchen table.

"That is about the size of it, and we would like your assistance in getting her back."

Sally poured boiling water from the kettle into two mugs containing generous amounts of instant coffee, stirred vigorously and took the mugs over to where the nun was sitting. After confirming that her companion did not want milk or sugar in her drink, they both sat down and sipped at the warm caffeine-rich brew.

"So what makes you think she has been abducted, or even worse?"

"Well, it's like this, you see. She didn't make contact at the prearranged time this evening. Without wanting to give away any operational details, every evening if things were all right she would leave a sign in an agreed place and one of our field operatives would check and report back to us at the HQ. Unfortunately this evening no such sign was found and we have not been able to contact her at the Dog and Duck – the landlord says she has not been back since she left for work that morning."

Sally held the coffee mug in both hands and could feel its comforting warmth as the caffeine did its job of slowly de-fogging her brain.

"Are you sure she has not just taken the night off or forgotten to check in? It could happen."

The nun frowned slightly at the thought.

"No, she is highly trained and too well-disciplined for that. Besides, we have picked up a signal from her tracking device within the grounds of High Meadow Manor and her car is still at the office where she parked it."

"I see, it is a tragic thing to happen but I am not sure exactly how we can help, surely this is a case for trained professionals such as yourselves?"

The nun looked deep into the depths of her coffee cup searching for the right words to convince the civilian sitting opposite her that she could play her part in getting Emma safely back and helping to rid the world of this latest dastardly plot by the forces of evil.

Her organisation did not usually ask for outside help but on this occasion it was unavoidable. "Usually I would agree with you. This is a matter that would normally be best left to the professionals, but due to your previous experience with Mr Di-Ablo, it was thought that both you and Freddy would be well placed to help us to get Emma back. Besides, you do have some assets in place that would be very useful to us."

Sally thought about what was being said. It was true she had helped foil the last plot by Vynce Di-Ablo, it had been a close run thing and she really didn't want to push her luck a second time, but deep down she knew that she couldn't stand by and do nothing. Surely it was her moral duty to give whatever help she could to free the kidnapped agent.

"I am not sure what we could possibly offer your organisation, but carry on, I'm listening."

Slowly things started to come into focus and she could just make out some high pitched chattering in the gloom. The chattering came from two Piskies who had been given orders to watch over Emma and notify Vynce when she regained consciousness, but who were instead busy cheating each other at cards. Emma sat up as her eyes adjusted to the gloom. Some weak light was starting to make its way through the ill-fitting planks of the barn. It must be the dawn breaking – had she really been out that long? She checked her arms and legs, good there were no restraints that she could see, that would help in any escape attempt.

Alerted by her movements, the Piskies stopped their game and walked over to where Emma was now sat on a bale of hay.

"Good morning, Miss Emma. I hope you slept well?"

Emma looked at the two elven-like figures that were now

standing in front of her. Both were wearing white lab coats with the Di-Ablo Enterprises logo on the breast pocket. The one that was speaking had a more confident air about him and seemed to be in charge while the other just looked at her with contempt.

Trying to give her best appearance of innocent confusion she looked soulfully at her two captors.

"Good morning to you too. What is going on? Did I have a bit too much to drink last night and pass out here in the barn? I really can't remember. Any way I must be going, I don't want to be late for work."

She stood up and started to head for the door. The two Piskies barred her way. Despite their diminutive size they made an intimidating sight and in her still slightly groggy state she hesitated momentarily, unsure what to do.

"I wouldn't do that if I were you, Miss Emma. Terrence is standing guard outside with orders to keep you here, and you know what a stickler for obeying orders he is. We have been asked to let Vynce know as soon as you regained consciousness, so we will be off now to tell him you are back with us. If I was you I would have a bit of breakfast and think about what you are going to say to Vynce. There is a sandwich and a bottle of water over there."

With that the two jailers left the barn. Emma took a peak through one of the knotholes in the planks that made up the outer skin of the barn and could see Terrence standing guard. She sat back down on the hay bale and looked at the curled up sandwich on the plate. Getting out of there may be a little more difficult than she had first thought.

Normally Freddy would have gone for the healthier muesli for breakfast but today he had chosen the less heathy option of a bacon sandwich. He took a bite and felt its smoky flavour excite his taste buds as a little bit of bacon grease dribbled down his chin. In that brief moment all of his cares had evaporated and all was once again right with the world. His unhealthy choice of breakfast had been prompted by the news given to him by his wife and the nun sat at his kitchen table about the part he was going to play in what seemed to him to be a foolhardy plan to rescue the undercover operative from the clutches of Vynce Di-Ablo. Muesli may be the way to a long heathy life, but as he saw it if your life is going to be cut short by a reckless mission, the breakfast of choice would have to be a bacon sandwich with just a hint of brown sauce. Now that he had the calming influence of the bacon grease and brown sauce infusion flowing through his veins he felt better able to cope with what was being said, and besides, with a bit of luck the cholesterol would clog his heart long before the mission even got under way.

"Could you run through the plan again, I am not totally sure I understand."

Sally went over the plan once more. As far as plans go it was a little light on detail, but it was quite simple and a little daring. They would snatch Emma back from right under the noses of Vynce Di-Ablo and his minions.

Freddy chewed the last mouthful of his breakfast and reluctantly nodded his approval.

In the barn, Emma chewed the last mouthful of her stale, curled up cheese and tomato sandwich and washed it down with a mouthful of the bottled water. It had looked unappetising and tasted little better, but she knew she needed to keep her strength up and did not know when she would get the opportunity to eat again. That was something else they had taught her at the academy, when in a tight spot like this take what was on offer as it might not be offered again. Another thing they had drummed into her was to stay calm and don't panic. Take stock of the situation and make an inventory of everything around you, no matter how small, as it might turn out to be useful.

Walking around the inside of the barn to make her inventory, she could see that there were bales of hay that had been piled up down one side in a half-hearted attempt to hide the many two-hundred litre drums of chemicals that seemed to be the main commodity stored there.

She moved one of the hay bales aside and could see the label on the drum, the chemical had an unpronounceable name but she knew it was not good to be around as it also had a large biohazard sticker on it and underneath this it had the words 'PROPERTY OF THE MOD' stencilled in large yellow letters. This was the same stuff she had seen being added to the fermentation vessels during her site tour. A plan formed in her mind, if she could destroy the drums, perhaps in a fire, it would prevent the production of any more of the mind-bending cider. It would be at a great risk to herself as she would certainly not survive the resulting inferno but at least the rest of humanity might stand a chance. Unfortunately her inventory had also revealed that there was no obvious way of starting a fire. Although a non-smoker she usually kept a book of matches in her bag for emergencies, but unfortunately her bag was nowhere to be seen, it must have been confiscated along with her phone and car keys when she was abducted.

Sitting on a hay bale as far away from the drums of chemicals as she could in the confined space, she was just wondering if it was actually possible to start a fire by rubbing two sticks together when the barn door opened and a car drove in. It was her car. The driver's door opened and the tall intimidating figure of Vince Di-Ablo extracted himself from the car's tiny interior and stood menacingly in front of her.

"Hi, Emma, I hope your being here is not too much of an inconvenience for you, but I think you know why you are here!"

Emma stayed seated and once again put the expression of confused innocence back on her face.

"I am not sure what you mean. Have I done something to offend you? Has my work not come up to your expectations? If not I am sure the agency could send someone else who would be a better fit in your organisation."

He looked down at the sad face of the woman who until recently had been his PA, the person whom he had trusted with the innermost secrets of his organisation. As a demon he was by default angry, but the thought of this betrayal made him even angrier. He fought down his increasing rage in an effort to remain calm, there would be time to get his revenge on her and her kind once he had taken over the world and crushed all his opposition. It was a day he looked forward to and that day would be soon.

"Come now, Emma, don't try that pitch with me. We both know which agency sent you and it wasn't the one that supplies high quality office staff; it was those goody two shoes God botherers who keep trying to stop me and my kin from taking our rightful place as the rulers of the planet and of all humanity. But this time it is too late, I will succeed. The product works and is proving to be a success, we have stepped up production and are taking it nationwide, in a month or so we will be global. Once we have the majority of the world hooked, humanity will be too weak to resist my takeover, and there is nothing you or your organisation can do to stop me."

The expression on Emma's face hardened.

"Don't underestimate us, Vynce. We have a team working day and night on trying to stop you and every piece of information I passed onto them makes them a step closer to shutting you down. Nothing that happens to me now can change that."

"I am sorry you see it that way. You and your colleagues will not succeed; my only regret will be that you will not be around long enough to witness first-hand my success."

He beckoned to the two Piskies that had been standing in the open doorway. They moved forward aggressively and looked threateningly at Emma.

"You have until sunset to change your mind and tell me everything you know about your organisation and any possible threat they may be to my plan. If after this time you still want to persist in playing the hero, my two friends here will organise a little accident for you. It is surprising how many cars lose control on these winding country roads and end up in ditches, and it can be days before they are found. So think on it."

It was dark and past midnight as Sally reversed the Land Rover and horse box through the open gate and into the paddock where Flotsam and Jetsam were resting. When they had taken over the farm they had been told by one of the regulars down at the Dog and Duck that it was written into the countryside code that all farms must have an old beaten up Land Rover on site at all times, even if it was not functional. Believing everything they had been told, they had abandoned their plans to scrap the aged off-roader that had been rusting silently in the barn when they bought the farm and instead had it restored to its former glory, with one exception. In an attempt to go green and reduce the amount of carbon dioxide produced by the off-roader, they had it converted to run on electricity. The work had been done by the local blacksmith cum car mechanic, who had replaced the old fossil fuel burning engine with the motor and batteries from an old electric forklift truck that, by coincidence, he had knocking about in his workshop. It wasn't fast but at least it was a bit more environmentally friendly. More importantly it was almost silent, something that would be an advantage for tonight's venture.

The two Shetland ponies had at first been startled by the appearance of the horsebox in their paddock, but they calmed down as they saw Sally approach them. Usually after dark they were left to their own devices, the only humans they saw were the occasional poacher on the hunt for rabbits. Tonight they could sense things were going to be different. Sally approached the ponies and slipped on their harnesses. Stroking them tenderly on the neck she whispered, "Hi Flotsam, hi Jetsam. I have a little job for you tonight so I need you to be on your best behaviour and do as your Auntie Sally tells you."

The two ponies exchanged a glance and followed Sally obediently into the waiting horse box.

They were a little confused at first, as normally a trip in the horse box meant a visit to a horse show or village fete where they would strut around in a ring and generally show off, hopefully winning a nice-coloured rosette in the process. Tonight though was different.

There had not been the usual hours spent grooming in preparation for the show and importantly it was dark, they had never gone to a show at this time of night before. As they walked, Sally explained to them exactly what she wanted them to do that night and as they liked Sally a great deal they decided to cooperate.

It was well past the deadline that Vynce had set and nothing much had happened in her wooden jail. Terrence still patrolled diligently up and down in front of the barn making sure that nothing and no one got past him that wasn't permitted. More than once he had reprimanded a field mouse for trying to enter the barn without proper authorisation or paperwork. Inside the barn Emma sat quietly contemplating her fate. She had abandoned her attempt to light a fire by rubbing two sticks together, as she had only managed to get the wood lukewarm and in the process got some nasty blisters on her hands. Vynce had been back to try and tempt her over to his team, but after an ill-tempered and acrimonious exchange he had left with his mood fouler than ever. She fiddled with her earrings; they were quite big and a little unfashionable for the younger woman, but a necessary part of her equipment as an agent in the field. Each earring contained a GPS tracker that continuously relayed her position back to the operations room so they could keep an eye on her movements at all times. It was reassuring to know that the guys back at the office knew where she was, she just wished they would hurry up and break her out before it was too late.

Silently, with its headlights switched off, the Land Rover and horse box made its way up the deserted farm track deep into the grounds of High Meadow Manor. It was a dark night with clouds preventing any illumination by moonlight. Through the night vision goggles, supplied curtesy of the nocturnal visiting nun, both Sally and Freddy had a clear view of the track ahead and the surrounding landscape.

"It looks like we are here, there's the gate."

Freddy stopped the car and looked around. In the distance he could make out the outline of a barn. Hopefully if their navigation was correct it should be the right one.

They got out of the Land Rover and walked up to the gate. Freddy adjusted the zoom function on his goggles and focused in on the barn and the huge troll that guarded it. He spoke softly to Sally and the nun who were also busy observing the barn.

"That must be where they are keeping her. Look at the size of the guard, he is enormous, are you sure we can get past him?"

The nun checked the screen on the GPS tracker.

"Yes, that is where she is. The guard is a troll called Terrence. He is quite big even by troll standards, but like everyone he has his weaknesses. Now come on, let's get the ponies unloaded."

Freddy reversed the horsebox through the open gate. Sally and the nun then led the ponies from the horse box and made them stand quietly in the entrance to the field.

"Now, Freddy, Sally and I are going to get into position, when we give the signal remember what you need to do."

"Of course, I do, no problem. You go and get in position and I'll wait here with the engine running."

Creaking slightly on its rusty hinges the door of the barn slowly opened. In the gloom Emma could make out the shapes of her two Piskie jailers as they walked menacingly towards her, Terrence loitering just outside. She could see that the Piskies were each holding something in their hand. Instinctively she ran towards the open doorway, digging her feet into the earthen floor of the barn to get better traction. Surprised by her sudden dash for freedom, the two Piskies stood rooted to the spot as she rushed by them, but Terrence was more alert, and as she ran through the door and out of the barn he swooped down with one of his large hands and scooped Emma up into the night air, ending her bid for freedom.

Making their way stealthily towards the barn dressed in

80

black boiler suits and wearing balaclavas, both Sally and the nun had seen the Piskies approach the barn and Emma's desperate bid for freedom. The nun signalled for Sally to stop. They were not quite as close as she would have liked, but time was running out, they would have to act now. She pressed the coms button on her radio to alert Freddy that it was time for him to act.

Freddy acknowledged the signal and turned to the ponies. "You know what you need to do."

With that he slapped them both on the rump and they rushed off into the darkness of the field towards the barn and the scent of the fresh hay they had been promised.

Recovering from their initial shock, the Piskies made their way over to where Emma was now dangling by one arm from the oversized hand of Terrence. The more senior of the two raised his arm, switched on his torch and shone its powerful beam into Emma's eyes, blinding her and depriving her of any night sight she may have had.

"That was a foolish thing to do, Emma! Do you really think you can escape? There is a lot of open countryside here and Terrence can cover a lot of ground. If you comply things will be very quick and painless. If, however, you choose to resist, my colleague here has something that will make you think again."

On cue the more junior of the two pressed the button on his cattle prod.

Still blinded, Emma heard the crackle of the electricity arcing between the electrodes of the cattle prod and she felt the fight leave her body.

Out in the darkness of the field the two figures in black boiler suits had resumed their stealthy approach towards the barn. In the gloom Sally could hear the hooves of Flotsam and Jetsam galloping towards the barn and the promise of fresh hay.

Terrence also heard the approach of thundering hooves and swung around to see what was going on and was amazed to see two delightful little ponies racing towards him. The ponies reminded him of a time, many years ago when he was younger and didn't have many friends and his parents had given him a pony as a present one birthday. He had loved that pony and they had spent many a happy time playing in the fields around where he lived.

Seeing the two ponies reminded him of those halcyon days, and forgetting where he was he released Emma from his grip and went running off to play with them. The ponies on their part saw the huge beast running towards them, turned and started to run as fast as they could in the opposite direction.

Momentarily on the back foot, the Piskies were unaware of the two figures in black boiler suits that were now right behind them and getting ready to pounce. It was Emma who gained her composure first and saw her rescue party approaching. In an effort to draw the attention of the Piskies away from their impending fate she stood up and dusted herself down.

"OK. You win. I have changed my mind, I will tell Vynce everything I know."

Feeling part pleased and part relieved, the Piskies made their way towards Emma. Unlike demons, Piskies are mischievous by nature but are very rarely malevolent and in fairness they had not been happy about carrying out the plan to eliminate the human and were pleased she had decided to cooperate. The feeling of relief was short lived however as they soon found themselves pinned to the ground under the weight of Sally and the nun. After a brief struggle the nun had used her combat training and managed to subdue and handcuff her target, while Sally on the other hand was struggling with hers. Although small, Piskies are very strong for their size and easily a match for the average human. Sally lost her grip on her target and he got up to run away, then there was a short crackle of electricity and he fell back down to the ground stunned. Sally looked up to see Emma standing over the dazed body of the Piskie with a cattle prod in her hand.

Further out in the darkness of the field, Terrence stopped and lay down on the grass exhausted and gasping in great lungfuls of air in an effort to get his breath back. He was disappointed. No matter how hard he had tried to play with them the ponies kept running away.

At a safe distance away, Flotsam and Jetsam had also stopped to get their breath back. They had been startled when the big creature had stared to run towards them and had no intention of getting near it so they had kept running back and forth until the creature had finally given up the chase. They felt lucky that they were faster and more agile than their pursuer.

At the gate, Freddy with the aid of his night vision goggles could see the figures of Sally, Emma and the nun heading back towards him at a great pace. He picked up the bucket containing Flotsam and Jetsam's favourite feed and rattled it loudly. Hearing the sound, the ponies pricked up their ears and also started to run towards the gate and their reward for a good night's work.

Chapter Ten

The first glow of dawn was starting to break on the horizon as Vynce Di-Ablo surveyed the scene of the night's jailbreak. He should have known better than to trust the Piskies with the disposal of that spy in the camp, Emma, but he could not do everything himself. That's why he had hired the Piskies in the first place, so that he could delegate the day to day tasks to them and get on with the important business of taking over the world. As for Terrence, how could such a large intimidating troll allow himself to be side tracked like that, and by small Shetland ponies! He had made his feelings clear when he had spoken with him.

A dejected Terrence sat on the hay bales in the barn reflecting on the night's events. He did not take rejection or criticism very well and was sitting there silently, his mind festering away. How could the ponies have been so horrid and refuse to play with him, and as for the reprimand he had received from Mr Di-Ablo it seemed so unfair, he had done a good job up until now keeping out unwanted intruders and doing all the fetching and carrying. It had been the best job he had ever had, but now it was tainted, so perhaps he should look for other employment. Perhaps if he asked nicely Mr Di-Ablo would give him a reference.

Sitting on a hay bale a little further down from Terrence was a Piskie swigging brandy from a hip flask, staring off into space and occasionally twitching involuntarily as electrical sparks jumped from his body out into the moist dawn air.

Jack the Lantern walked up to where Vynce was standing.

He had carried out a detailed search of the area but had come up with very little evidence of who the culprits were, although after a previous conversation Vynce seemed to have a good idea who was behind it.

"Excuse me, sir."

Vynce looked down at Jack. He was one of the more senior and reliable of the Piskies and he valued his opinion.

"Hello, Jack. I hope you have some good news for me?"

"Not much I am afraid, sir. I have had a good look at the area and it would appear that there were three perpetrators and two Shetland ponies involved in this, which is as much as we already knew. They came and left down the old track over there that runs through the estate, in a four by four towing a horse box. The tyre tracks are most likely from a Land Rover or similar vehicle, a common enough vehicle type around these parts. We have traced the tracks back out to the road but there is no indication of which way they went after that. All in all there is very little to go on I am afraid, sir."

Vynce listened to what Jack was telling him and fought to supress the anger that was again growing inside of him.

"Thank you, Jack. I suspect the people that did this were very careful to cover their tracks. No matter, this will not deflect us from our task, we will just need to be a bit more careful and speed up our plans a little, that's all. I want round the clock security patrols of the whole estate with an emphasis on the manufacturing facility, and I want production stepped up so we run twenty-four-seven, is that clear? And tell Terrence he is not to play with any more ponies!"

Jack acknowledged the instructions and headed off to make the arrangements.

The mood around the kitchen table was ebullient as Sally and Freddy recalled the night's heroic deeds and how they had overcome the odds to rescue Emma from her fate. Emma on the other hand was a bit more subdued; she had been extremely close to meeting a premature end and the thought kept playing through her mind. Against the advice of her colleague, Emma had refused to go back to headquarters for a debriefing but had instead told the nun everything she knew about Di-Ablo enterprises and the plot to take over the world and had decided to stay on site to finish the job. Much to Freddy's dismay, Sally had insisted that Emma should stay with them and use the farm as a base for her operations.

Freddy on the other hand had thought that they had done their bit and it was up to the 'organisation' to finish up the job and leave them free to get on with the task of growing food for the nation. Emma made her excuses and headed upstairs for a shower that she hoped would remove the smell of musty hay that had worked its way into her clothes and seemed to be lingering in her hair.

Now safely back in their paddock, Flotsam and Jetsam, a little weary from their night time exertions, stood quietly in the field and nibbled on a patch of sweet clover.

"Ladies, if I could have your attention for a moment."

The chatter around the table subsided into silence. Dora looked around at the other eleven witches who were seated around the conference table in Vynce's office. To her right at the head of the table sat a very agitated and grumpy Vince Di-Ablo.

"Our lord and master Vyncent Di-Ablo has called us here this morning as he would like our help in identifying the enemies of his, and for that matter ours, that last night broke into these sacred grounds in an attempt to subvert his great work and violate his will."

At the sound of the word violate one of the witches started to giggle. Vynce fixed her with an unyielding stare and she fell silent.

"As you know, he is all powerful, but with our help his power is boundless so I would like you all to pledge an oath to help him root out and destroy his enemies."

A chorus of "we so pledge" ran around the table.

A slightly placated Vynce Di-Ablo got to his feet and addressed the assembled coven.

"As you may or may not be aware, a day or so ago we discovered there was a traitor in our midst. This treacherous conspirator was sent by our enemies not only spy on us but to try and stop me becoming your one true leader. Due to our constant vigilance this collaborator was caught before they could do any damage, but unfortunately, with a little outside help they managed to escape before we could teach them the error of their ways.

"With the help of Dora here I have searched the ether and ascertained that the traitor is nearby, perhaps still in the village. Now with your combined power focused through this crystal ball I should be able to home in and locate the perpetrator of this crime and those who may harbour our enemy."

A ripple of applause ran around the table. Then at Vynce's command they all linked hands, bowed their heads and concentrated their inner energy towards the crystal ball.

The ethereal mist in the crystal swirled and eddied within the sphere, ebbing and flowing until it slowly cleared to show three figures seated around a farmhouse table, one man and two women. Focusing the energy from the coven, Vynce zoomed in on the three figures until he could see their faces. The first one he recognised as Emma, his ex-PA. The images of the man and the other woman were however fainter and fuzzier, like an out of focus photograph. He concentrated more power into the orb but their energy was hard to read.

Slowly with the crystal now at its maximum power capacity the final two faces came into focus and he was shocked by what he saw looking back at him. He recognised them; it had been a year or two since he had last seen them and they had aged a little, but it was them all right, Freddy Brown and his partner in crime Sally. Freddy had been the chief scientist on his last attempt to subvert humanity and all had been going well until Freddy had become besotted with Sally and she and her accomplices had convinced him to join forces and foil the plot. This time though it would be different, this time he knew who they were and in a moment he would know their exact location. He focused a bit more but the vision was slowly fading into a dot until it had gone completely and the crystal was clear once more. Damn, he was so close to finding them.

Looking up at the figures around the table he could see the reason for the loss of transmission; one of the witches, Muriel, if he remembered correctly was fidgeting about and looking at her watch. He fixed her with a firm stare.

"Hi, Muriel, is there a problem?"

Muriel stopped fidgeting and tried to avoid his gaze.

"Will we be much longer? Only my Collin is stuck in bed with a bad back and I promised I would be back in time to change his poultice and get him a bit of dinner."

Fighting back his anger, he put a thin smile on his face and made a mental note to use his demonic powers to sort out Collin's back problems on a permanent basis. At least he now knew who he was dealing with and now he knew who they were, there were other earthlier ways to locate them.

"No, Muriel, that's fine, you go on back to Collin. I have enough information for now."

In the kitchen of Rose Well Farm, a freshly showered Emma had joined Freddy and Sally for a cup of tea and breakfast. Sally had lent her some fresh clothes until her own possessions could be retrieved safely from her room at the Dog and Duck. She placed a briefcase on the table, set the code on the combination locks and clicked the lid open. The briefcase had been left by her colleague and contained a myriad of gadgets and equipment that an operative in the field might need. After rummaging around for a moment or two she pulled out three rather large and ugly looking necklaces, she kept one and handed the other two to Sally and Freddy.

Freddy looked at the strange piece of jewellery. Dangling on the end of a substantial silver chain was a round silver disc with a diameter similar to that of his tea mug, and in the centre there was set a large turquoise stone and around this there were four smaller orange stones set at equally spaced intervals. He was not one for jewellery, the only jewellery he wore was the wedding ring on his finger, but even to his untrained eye this piece of jewellery was not something that would ever be called fashionable. In fact he thought it was quite hideous. "You're not expecting me to wear that, are you?"

Emma put hers around her neck and gestured for Sally and Freddy to do the same.

"They may not look very elegant but they are a first line of defence against the forces of evil, so I suggest you put it on."

Freddy was unconvinced.

"It is just a bunch of coloured stones attached to a lump of metal that's hanging on a chain. How can it protect us from evil?"

"It may look a little odd but the technology behind it is very old and very reliable. I can't tell you exactly how it works, but the basic version is this; the small orange stones act as antennae that detect any supernatural energy that may be generally in the ether or specifically aimed at you. This information is fed to the central turquoise stone that identifies the energy type, disables any malevolent intent and then converts the bad energy into heat that is then dissipated by the metal disk. Worn around the neck it can prevent demons from looking into your mind and will make you almost impossible to detect by telepathy or crystal ball. It is basically stealth technology against the forces of evil."

In unison both Sally and Freddy hung the medallions around their necks. Freddy tucked his inside his shirt in an attempt to hide it from view. It may help protect him from demons but he knew there would be some serious questions from Ted and Jed if they saw it. As the medallion made its way down his shirt and the metal touched his skin, instead of the expected feel of cold metal the medallion felt warm to the touch, not uncomfortably hot, just a little above body temperature.

Chapter Eleven

In the days following Emma's escape, things had started moving at pace at Di-Ablo enterprises. Production was running twenty-four-seven, and pallets of the psychotropic cider were piling up in the warehouse. Contracts had been signed by pub chains, off-licences and supermarkets alike, and adverts were running on commercial television and radio twenty-four-seven to sell this latest designer cider to the mass market. Pleased by the progress, his mood had lightened slightly and Vynce was almost back to his usual level of demonic grumpiness.

Using just one finger he poked awkwardly at the keys on the keyboard and clicked the mouse buttons until the screen displayed what he was looking for. It was an online news service provider, he scrolled through the headlines until he found what he was after. It was a roundup of some of the lesser news stories from around the country, stories that were not quite headline material but instead provided some light relief from the usual gloom and doom stories that were preferred by the nation's news editors. Carefully he scrolled through the stories checking every last detail such as names, locations, times and dates. There were all manner of strange things happening all over the country; there was a tale of a man from East Anglia that had built a scale model of the Tower of London from root vegetables, then there was the strange case of the group of businessmen who had abandoned their high level business negotiations to go outside and howl at the full moon, the article finished with a story of a man from

Milton Keynes who had planted a flag in the middle of a roundabout and claimed it for the British Empire. Vynce sat back and allowed himself a little smile; he had managed to create all of this mayhem from the comfort of his own office in just a few short minutes with nothing more than a crystal ball and some psychotropic cider. He had been proud of the last one; it had a sort of irony about it. For once his plan was working, he was now able to control the minds of whoever drank his evil brew and within a few days he would have control of enough minds to throw first the country and then the world into chaos. Then he would plant his flag upon the earth and claim it for himself. So pleased was he with his success that he had almost forgotten that he had so far been unable to track down the whereabouts of his traitorous PA and her helpers. But to his way of thinking he was so far down the road now that there was very little that could be done to stop him.

Sitting at the kitchen table of Rose Well Farm, Emma looked at the laptop screen, and peering back at her were the faces of the others participants of the video conference. Some of the faces she recognised as colleagues from headquarters, others were disguising their identities with masks, and she could see two Margret Thatchers and one Ronald Reagan in amongst the crowd. These she thought must be the shadowy top level figures that directed policy and operations; their use of disguises from long forgotten celebrities rather than those of more modern personalities was an indication of their age and time in the job.

Huddled behind her were Freddy, Sally, Ted and Jed.

Ted looked at the screen in amazement. It was the first time he had seen anything like it. He had heard rumours about the advances in technology that allowed you to make phone calls face-to-face, but by and large the digital age had passed him by. He had no need for computers or the internet, all the knowledge he needed was tucked away inside his head and if ever he had a work related problem that he could not overcome himself, he would go and see one of the other local farmers and between them they could usually sort it out over a pint down at the Dog and Duck. When they had bought the new tractor it had come with built in GPS and computer software that would tell them exactly where to apply more fertiliser or spray for pests, but he never had a need to use it. He had worked the land for many years just like his father and grandfather before him and knew instinctively what the yields were for each field and what to do to get the best efficiency from the land. His main concession to modern technology was a television set that he used to get the long range weather forecast to help him plan the week ahead and also for his wife to watch all of the soap operas.

Jed however was a little more comfortable with this new technology. He had in pride of place in his cottage an ancient laptop that had been given to him by his cousin when she decided to shun the rural way of life and leave the village and had migrated to London.

Every week he would log on using his neighbour's internet connection and have a video call with her and catch up with all the latest fads and fashions that were happening in the big city. He marvelled at her stories of trains that ran in tunnels under the city streets, the grand theatre productions and of the eclectic mix of foods and cultures that existed side by side on London's busy streets. So impressed was he by these tales that he had made it his life's ambitions to one day take the coach to London and try one of those kebabs for himself.

As the meeting progressed the mood around the table

became more and more sombre as the enormity and seriousness of the task that lay ahead slowly sank into them. This was probably the most serious crisis that had faced humankind for many decades, if not centuries, and they were on the front line, success or failure rested on their shoulders.

After timetables and task allocations had been agreed, the meeting broke up and the video call was disconnected. Emma tapped on the keyboard of the laptop, erasing any record of their call from the various registers and logs before switching it off and closing the lid.

Freddy ran his fingers through his thinning hair, what he had just heard and signed up to during the call chilled him to the core and the thought that he and his friends in the room held the future course of humanity in their hands sent a shiver down his spine. He needed something to bring him back to normality and keep him there.

"I don't know about anyone else but I could do with a coffee, does anyone else want one?"

After draining their coffee cups, Ted and Jed made their excuses and headed out to the barn where the tractor and Land Rover were plugged in and charging, filling their batteries with the electrons lovingly harvested from the sun's powerful rays. After making doubly sure that the vehicles were plugged in and charging, a serious looking Ted placed his hand on Jed's shoulder and said, "Make sure that these are kept fully charged at all times. This is one job that Hercules won't be able to help us with."

Sitting at his desk, Vynce looked at the latest sales and marketing information, things looked good. His cider was now the top selling brand in the country and was making excellent inroads overseas. Everything was coming together nicely – he would act soon. He pulled up the calendar on his computer screen and tapped at a date on the monitor and smiled a thin smile. That would do nicely, very nicely indeed. The thirty-first of October, it would be the final irony; the one day in the year when the spirits were supposed to walk the earth among the humans would be the day he took it over. The day would go down in history and be remembered throughout all the galaxies in all the dimensions in all of the universes as the day that he, Vyncent Di-Ablo, outwitted the forces of good and enslaved humanity to his will.

Sally supervised Ted and Jed as they unloaded a wooden crate from the back of a Morris Minor Traveller that had pulled up in the stable yard and carried it over to the stables. After they had carefully set it down on the floor, Sally unhooked a crowbar from a nail in one of the wooden posts that held up the roof of the stables and set about opening the crate.

Ted looked at the contraption that had been in the crate, took off his cloth cap and scratched his head. It was another wooden box, but this one was made of highly polished mahogany. At one end of the box there was a long wiring harness several metres in length that was terminated with a connector not dissimilar to the one the tractor used to connect it to the charging point. At the other end there were two thick cables, one red and the other green, each cable terminated with a heavily insulated spring loaded clamp. In the middle of the box sat a thick brass double pole knife switch of a type favoured by eccentric Victorian inventors to power up their latest creations. Also in the crate were a cordless angle grinder and a small instruction booklet. Ted looked at it all; he was getting outside of his comfort zone and was a little confused. How was this going to stop the big wig at the manor house taking over the world, perhaps they were going to throw it at him and hope he would run away?

Sally, seeing Ted's confusion, picked up the instruction booklet and handed it to him.

"Have a look through this and familiarise yourself with it, and meet me in the conservatory in half an hour, and don't forget to lock the stable door. We don't want it to go missing."

Half an hour later Ted and Jed joined Sally, Freddy and Emma in the conservatory. Ted held his cap in his hands and eyed the plants suspiciously, they eyed him back. It was not that he had anything against them, he was happy to take care and water them while Freddy and Sally were away, it was just that he could not get used to them talking back to him or telling him off when he overwatered them. He had spent all his life in and around farming growing all types of crops, and had not up until recently realised that the plants he had been growing all these years for food had feelings too and that thought made him uneasy around Freddy's genetically enhanced collection of flora.

Emma moved the coffee cups aside and put a hand drawn map on the table.

"Our intelligence suggests that Vynce will probably make his move to try and take over the world tonight as it is Halloween, so we need to act quickly to prevent him from putting his plan into action. If you could all look at the map I will run through the actions we need to take to stop him."

She then proceeded to go over the final plan with her assembled troops, pointing to the various targets of interest and who was doing what and when.

"Does anybody have any questions?"

There was an awkward silence in the conservatory. Being a practical man and still not exactly sure about what exactly the highly polished box with the cables was for, Ted broke the silence.

"I hate to appear a little slow on the uptake here but what is that gizmo in the stables going to do exactly once we get it in place?"

Emma looked into the face of the aging farm manager, she understood his concern, she had not been fully briefed on what the box did, she only knew what needed to be done with it. "I can appreciate your unease with this, Ted, but don't worry about it too much, as long as you and Jed can get it in position and operational at the right time that is all that is really needed. The techies back at base assure me it will work, so that is all I know."

Jed raised his hand. "Excuse me, Miss Emma, but did you say there were some of the fairy folk working up at the manor? I am not superstitious or anything but should we be messing with them? I hear that they can put a curse on you if you upset them."

"Again, I understand your concern, Jed. The Piskies can be a little mischievous when it comes to interacting with humans, but I am sure we will be safe from any curses."

Noting the scepticism in the faces of Jed and Ted, Emma reached into her briefcase and pulled out two amulets and handed one to each of them.

"Take these just in case and keep them on your person at all times. They will ward off any curses that the Piskies may try and put on you."

The two men eagerly took the jewelled charms and stuffed them in their pockets, satisfied with the knowledge that whatever else happened they would be safe from whatever the Piskies may throw at them.

On its stand next Freddy's chair, the leaves of Spathy the genetically modified peace lily rustled to gain attention and its flower slowly pulsed from white to orange and back to white again.

"Excuse me for interrupting but I have heard a bit of gossip from the whispering grass that the Piskies have been given the night off and are having a little bit of a Halloween party of their own over at the manor, so I don't think there will be any problems with them, Jed, in case you were still worried."

Jed nodded in the direction of Spathy.

"Thanks, Spathy. That information and the amulet makes me feel a lot happier. Life is tough enough without having a curse put on you by the little people."

With all the questions answered and everyone knowing what they had to do, the meeting broke up and they left the conservatory, each one lost in their own thoughts on how the events of the next few hours might unfold.

Chapter Twelve

Emma walked around the Land Rover and tractor that were lined up one behind the other in the stable yard and checked that all the equipment required for the night's operation had been packed and properly stowed. Satisfied that all was as it should be, she climbed into the driving seat of the Land Rover, put on her night vision goggles and with the headlights off headed out of the farm and onto the lane to the village, followed closely behind by Ted and Jed in the tractor.

When they got close to the village, Emma stopped the Land Rover and had a good look around using her night vision aids. All was quiet, most of the Halloween revelry was over and the villagers were now back in their homes behind closed curtains. The only movement was around the Dog and Duck where the last of the guests were being sent on their way by Dave the landlord. Satisfied that all was well, she pressed the coms button on her radio and spoke to Ted and Jed in the tractor.

"All looks quiet. There should not be any problems with you getting to your target, we are heading to ours. Don't forget, once you have completed your task, get out of there and head straight back to the rendezvous, we will meet you there."

Jed acknowledged the message and watched as the Land Rover silently and stealthily headed off towards its objective. He engaged the tractor's drive and just as silently headed out towards his own target.

In the canteen at Di-Ablo Enterprises, a party was in full

swing, there was music, dancing and much frivolity. The party was to celebrate the part they had played in Vynce's plan to take over the world and the elevation in status they had been promised in the new world order that would soon follow. For a long time they had hidden away, their role in the world undervalued especially by the humans. Now they were being given the opportunity to show what they could really do and perhaps even show the elves a thing or two.

The music came courtesy of a small Piskie band playing traditional toe-tapping Piskie tunes on a collection of old worn out instruments. The merriment was being fuelled by the large quantities of bootleg apple brandy that was being consumed by the revellers. Unbeknown to Vynce, the Piskies had appropriated some of the fermented apple juice before it had reached the stage where the nerve agent was added and had distilled it into a potent applejack brandy, as one of the elders had put it "a nice little bonus for all our hard work."

In a corner sat a slightly merry Terrence. He was not usually one for drink or parties, but after the events of the last few days he felt he needed something to perk him up a little and had jumped at the chance when the piskies invited him to their celebration bash. Unused to drinking, he had underestimated the strength of the applejack brandy and was feeling a little woozy and so had decided to sit down for a bit while the room stopped spinning. This had come as a bit of a relief to the Piskies as his clumsy attempts at dancing had shaken the foundations of the building, causing some of the musicians to be thrown off the makeshift stage, interrupting the flow of the evening's carousing.

Two floors above the party, Vynce sat in his darkened office, the noise below being attenuated by the fabric of the building to a dull hum. Now that the office had stopped shaking he could get on with the night's serious business of taking over the world. First he would take out the instruments of power such as the police and armed forces, making it difficult for any government to mount a serious challenge to his coup, and then he would control the minds of the masses causing them to rise up against their masters until all of the prime ministers, presidents, dictators and other leaders around the world bent to his demands, bowed down and acknowledged him as their one true all-powerful ruler. The world and all its riches would then be all his to do with as he pleased. The thought made him feel good.

There was a thump and the building shook slightly as Terrence passed out and fell off his chair. This sudden noise roused Vynce out from his thoughts and back to the reality of the present. To achieve his aim he would need a little help. Through the gloom he looked at Dora and her coven of witches who were assembled around the conference table. He would need all of their combined power tonight to put his plan into action so it was important that he had the complete concentration of all of those assembled around the table. To this end he had taken the precaution of casting a demonic spell to alleviate the back pain of Muriel's long suffering husband to ensure there were no interruptions.

He waved his hands over the crystal ball, the ethereal mist in the crystal swirled once again, ebbing and flowing inside the sphere. He gestured to those around the table to all link hands; he felt their collective energy surge through his body and he focused it through his mind and on into the crystal. Suddenly the mist in the ball cleared and he could clearly see the life force of the billions of humans that inhabited the earth, he could select each one at random and zoom into their minds and see their innermost thoughts. Good, this was just what he wanted, all he had to do now was focus in on those in law enforcement and the armed services that had imbibed his evil brew and he would be underway.

Heading down the main road in the village, Jed steered the tractor silently towards the church while Ted complained about the cramped conditions inside the cab and how the cable from the box gizmo was digging into his leg. Jed sympathised with his boss's complaint. Ordinarily the cab was spacious enough for him as he went about his duties on the farm, but now with Jed and that box of tricks on board things were cramped to say the least.

"Hold on, Ted, we are almost there. I can see the lych-gate coming up."

Jed stopped the tractor by the lych-gate. "I think we may have a problem."

"What do you mean?" replied a slightly irritated Ted who was now massaging his leg in an attempt to try and get the circulation going again.

"The gate! It is too small to get the tractor through. We need to find another way in."

Ted extricated himself from the cab and lowered himself to the ground. It was a fact all right; there was no way they could get their farm vehicle through there without damaging the recently restored entrance to the churchyard. As it was the vicar was not going to be best pleased with what they were about to do, so to keep him out the way he had been sent off to a meeting with the bishop to discuss ecclesiastical matters and would not be back until the morning.

Being a practical man, Ted soon came up with a solution to the predicament.

"No problem, Jed, just back up a little bit and we will go through the hedge and in that way. Be careful how you go and don't drive over any of the graves, my great uncle Septimus is buried over there and I don't want him complaining again. It took gallons of holy water and a load of bibles scattered around the house to get rid of him last time!"

Jed backed up and then pushed his way through the hedge which offered very little in the way of resistance to the weight and power of the agricultural vehicle.

Sitting in the back of the Land Rover, Freddy was starting to get a little nervous not only at the thought of what they were about to do, but also about the strong smell of petrol that was coming from the jerry cans packed in the luggage space of the car. Just one spark from a dodgy battery connection and they would be toast, quite literally, toast. He wound down his window to let in a bit of air, hoping it would be enough to reduce the fumes to a safe level.

They drove down the same track as they had the other night on the mission to rescue Emma and came to a stop at the gate as they had before. Looking through their night vision goggles, they scanned the surroundings for signs of activity. None were seen. Emma turned to face her companions.

"It looks like the coast is clear, no-one about, not even Terrence. The barn is completely unguarded."

She gently squeezed the accelerator and steered the Land Rover slowly and silently through the open gate and down towards the barn while Sally and Freddy scanned the area for signs of activity.

Outside the barn, Sally and Freddy busied themselves unloading the petrol-filled jerry cans from the back of the Land

Rover while Emma forced the flimsy padlock from the barn door with a crowbar. The barn had been less secure than she had thought, with just the one flimsy padlock to keep out unwanted visitors. Why install sophisticated security when you have a Terrence?

Once inside they sprinkled liberal amounts of petrol over the remaining barrels of nerve agent and the surrounding bales of hay. Any unused jerry cans were stacked around the nerve agent barrels for good measure.

Jed had managed to manoeuvre the tractor through the churchyard, taking care to miss Ted's great uncle's grave, and had parked it in the prearranged location. Ted was busy with the angle grinder cutting his way through the copper lightning conductor that protected the fabric of the church from electrical storms. Once through, he pulled apart the two ends of the copper conductor to give a safe air gap as he had been instructed by the manual and then used the angle grinder to polish the ends to get rid of the green Verdigris that coated the surface of the thick copper strip.

Jed unloaded the wooden box from the tractor's cab and carefully laid it on the ground, making sure that the knife switch was in the open position. Satisfied that all was as it should be and that the copper connections were clean and shiny, Ted went ahead and connected the two spring-loaded clamps to the lightning conductor, double checking that the red connection was attached to the copper strip that went up the side of the church to the top of the steeple and that the green clamp was connected to the part that was buried in the ground. Once the clamps were secure and Ted was safely out of the way, Jed went ahead and plugged the lead from the box into the tractor's power socket. Ted checked his watch – they were on schedule.

Outside the barn Emma, checked her watch. It was time. She pressed the coms button on her radio, checked that Ted and Jed were in position and then gave the command, "GO." Sally lit the wick on a Molotov cocktail and from a safe distance threw it into the barn. There was a satisfying whoosh as the petrol ignited and she could feel the air rush past her as it was sucked in towards the flames. She turned and ran to the open door of the Land Rover and got in just as Emma started to accelerate away. Even with its modifications, the Land Rover lived up to its reputation as an off-roader and accelerated effortlessly across the field and back up the track to the safety and anonymity of the public highway.

On the word "GO" Ted had closed the knife switch and watched in amazement as a huge surge of power made its way almost instantaneously from the tractor's battery through the box and up the lightning conductor, and in the darkness he could see the copper glow bright red as the electricity rushed on its way to the top of the spire. Once at the top, there was a deafening whump as the electrons leapt out from the weather vane on the top of the church spire in a massive electromagnetic pulse so powerful that the lead roofing of the spire melted with the heat, and in the night sky above the church the clouds under the influence of the wave formed into concentric rings which ran off into the distance like ripples on a pond.

Slightly dazed and a little deafened, Ted picked himself up off the ground where he had been deposited by the shockwave. He looked at the box; the knife switch had partially melted and was now welded in the "ON" position. Seeing the state of the switch, he felt pleased that he had taken the extra precautions of wearing his rubber chemical-proof gloves and wellies. Jed was giving the tractor a look over, the power meter on the dashboard was showing zero charge and he could feel the heat and smell the acrid chemical vapours wafting out from the destroyed battery pack, and wondered if they could get it repaired under warranty.

"It looks like we are going to have to walk back."

Ted took of his gloves and patted his friend on the shoulder.

"Don't worry about it, I will send Jethro and Hercules round in the morning to tow it back. Come on, let's get back to the farm, I could do with a drink."

Things were going to plan and Vynce was as happy as it is possible for a demon to be. The witches were concentrating hard and giving him all the power he needed to carry out his fiendish plan. He had managed to locate the senior commanders of the emergency services and armed forces and was in the process of neutralising their thought processes when he heard the whump of the electromagnetic pulse followed immediately by the rattling of the windows as the pressure wave from the electromagnetic pulse surged around the building. Undeterred, he carried on with his work unaware of the significance of the sound.

There was a slight time delay as the pulse worked its way out from the village church spire across the country, then out across the sea and further out to the rest of the world until the globe was wrapped in its electron-fuddled embrace.

One by one, the minds he was so carefully manipulating were shutting down their access to him as the pulse rolled over their locations and neutralised the effect of the psychotropic cider. Frantically he tried to re-establish contact only to be denied each time. What was happening? The connection was good and the power he had was more than enough to do the job, he could probe the minds but he had no control over them. Frustrated, he slammed his fist on the table and stood up, disturbing the concentration of the witches and disconnecting him from their source of power.

There was a fizzing of static as the witches unlinked their hands and started to massage the circulation back into them. Dora looked at Vynce and could see the anger that was building up inside of him.

"What's the matter, Vynce? What has happened?"

Vynce let out a mighty roar. "What has happened! They have gone and found a way to stop me, that is what has happened. All of this plotting and scheming for nothing. All my hard work turned to dust. I will find out who did this and I will have my revenge."

Scared by the rantings of their almighty master, all of the witches except for Dora hurriedly fled the room, frightened in case he took his anger out on them. He sat back down in front of the crystal ball, his anger starting to subside. Dora sat down next to him.

"How could they do that? You were so close and your power was so strong I would not have thought it possible."

Vynce concentrated his mind into the crystal, probing in every corner of the ether for answers. As he searched he could see the confusion in the minds of the humans as they tried to understand what had just happened and why the clouds looked so odd. Most were putting it down to a bad dream or some sort of alcohol-induced hallucination and were getting back on with their lives unaware of the catastrophe that had so nearly befallen them. After a few moments, tucked away at the back of the images and almost hidden by a wisp of ethereal mist, he could see a vision of two men, one older than the other, standing in the village churchyard next to a tractor that seemed to be smouldering. He didn't recognise them but surely this was no coincidence. A large electromagnetic pulse had been generated nearby and here were two men standing by the burned out remains of what appeared to be an electric tractor that was plugged into the church steeple, using it like a large antennae.

He stood up and strode purposefully out of the room and down the stairs to where the Piskie party was still going strong. The Piskies had been enjoying themselves so much that they were unaware of the pulse that had ruined Vynce's plan or the fire that was raging in the barn destroying the stocks of nerve agent at the heart of his evil brew. The first they knew of it was when Vynce threw open the canteen door and shouted for silence. The Piskies were silent, very silent.

An angry Vynce addressed the crowd.

"There are two men, locals I think, who are presently in the vicinity of the churchyard. I want you to go out, find them and bring them to me. They have some serious questions to answer."

Pleased with their night's work the occupants of the Land Rover headed back to the rendezvouses at the farm. Emma checked in with her bosses, all had gone to plan. There had been a few minor side effects with some television and radio signals being temporally disrupted by the magnetic pulse and there were some unconfirmed reports of rain drops starting to reverse course and head back up into the clouds, attracted by the strong static electrical force that had been induced in them by the pulse, but apart from that the initial intelligence was that Vynce had been denied his chance to interfere with humanity and that the clean-up operation could begin.

Silently, Ted and Jed slipped out over the back wall of the churchyard and out into the open countryside and hurriedly made their way back towards the farm, putting as much distance as they could between them and the now smouldering church spire. The lead that clad the spire had taken the full force of the energy pulse that surged up from the tractor's batteries and had melted slightly, making the very top third of the spire droop in a south-easterly direction. The vicar was not going to be pleased when he got back and saw that, thought Jed, as he looked back over his shoulder before catching up with Ted, who for a man of his age was making good progress across the ploughed field.

Once across the field they stopped by the boundary hedge to get their breath back. They could feel their hearts beating furiously inside their chests as they gulped in great lungfuls of the chilled night air. As their heart rates started to return to normal, Ted heard a buzz in the earpiece of his radio, and he pushed the button on the handset to answer the call. It was Emma checking in to make sure they were safe and heading back to the farm. He confirmed all was well and that they would be there shortly.

As they made their way down a bridleway that led out to the main road through the village, Jed stopped and held his hand up in a signal for Ted to stop.

"Can you hear that?"

"Hear what?"

"That rustling noise, it sounds like there is someone in the bushes!"

Ted stopped and strained his ears, listening for any unusual noises, but all he could hear was the constant hum of his tinnitus.

"I can't hear anything. Anyway, who would be out here in the middle of the night? It is probably a fox or a badger or some other creature of the night."

Jed conceded the point and took a step forward before stopping again, distracted by the faint glow of a light in the path in front of him.

Jed looked down to get a better look at the source of the eerie glow. As his eyes focused he could see that the glow was coming from an old fashioned looking candle lantern that was being held by a small elf-like creature. He had only heard stories about them, about how they would find lost travellers out on the moors at night and lead them astray, but he had never seen one in the flesh before. From its diminutive size, weather-worn face and the wispy white hair and pointed ears that protruded from under its cap, he recognised the being in front of him immediately as a Cornish Piskie.

Unaware of his companion's sudden stop, Ted had also resumed walking and strode straight into the back of Jed.

"What's going on? Why have you stopped? I could have done myself a mischief."

"Piskie!"

Ted regained his balance and looked at his friend.

"What's that you say 'Piskies'? Don't be daft, it's probably a badger or a hedgehog or something, now let's get going before someone sees us."

He started to make his way around Jed before stopping dead in his tracks as he too saw the wizened face of the Piskie illuminated by the eerie flickering light from the candle lamp. He slowly put his hand in his pocket and grasped the amulet that Emma had given him at their meeting. As he looked around he could see the shadows of many other Piskies encircling them. Instinctively he pulled out the amulet from his pocket and waved it in all directions at the figures that stood blocking their path.

Jack the Lantern stood his ground unimpressed by the two humans and looked curiously at the jewel in Jed's hand.

"It's no use trying to bribe us with that, we've already got a better offer, and just in case you were thinking that it was some sort of magical 'get out of jail free card' that would force us to run away, think again, that is just an old wives' tale. Now if you could just concentrate on the lamp here and follow me I am sure we could avoid a lot of unpleasantness."

Ted could feel his will to resist drain away as the urge to comply with the Piskie's request grew stronger. Just as the last reserves of his free will started to desert him, he managed to press the transmit button on his radio.

"MAYDAY, MAYDAY. HELP!"

Chapter Thirteen

They were just pulling into the stable yard of Rose Well Farm when Ted's Mayday came through on the radio. Performing a handbrake turn, Emma slid the Land Rover through one-hundred and eighty degrees and accelerated back down the farm track towards the village. As she drove, she prodded at the screen of the smartphone that was in a cradle fixed to the dashboard of the car. After a momentary pause the display on the screen changed to show a map of the village and two flashing dots. One dot was the location of the Land Rover, the other showed the position of Ted and Jed. Their position was being transmitted by the amulets that both men had in their pockets. She had known when she had given them the amulets that they were really tracking devices and would not have any effect on the Piskies – it had been more of a confidence booster to take their minds off of the Piskie situation – but now she was glad they had them. As the Land Rover bounced at speed down the farm track, she prayed she could get to them in time.

Mesmerised by the hypnotic fumes from the candle lamp, both Ted and Jed complied and followed Jack the Lantern down the bridle path and out onto the road that ran through the village. Parked in a layby opposite the bridle path was a large dark car with a custom paint job of hot rod flames flowing out from the front wheel arches and over the front doors. The rear door of the car opened and the two men obediently got in and sat on the back seat.

In the front of the car were two human-like figures, one small with wispy white hair and pointed ears that stuck out from underneath his chauffeur's cap, the other was tall, muscular and had a more imposing presence. The taller of the two turned around to look at Ted and Jed who were now sat on the back seat, guarded by a number of menacing looking Piskies.

"Good morning, gentlemen, I am sorry if we have inconvenienced you, but if you can answer some questions we can get this over with nice and quick and you will both be on you way."

Ted shifted in his seat, squashing one of his guards against the closed door of the car. The hypnotic effects of the candle fumes were starting to wear off and his mind was slowly beginning to reboot. He looked across at Jed who was also starting to stir, and then looked in the direction of the voice that seemed to be speaking to him.

"What's that you say?"

Vynce looked at the older of the two men and felt some dismay that his fool-proof scheme to take over the world had been sabotaged by these two ordinary-looking humans.

"I am in a hurry so I will cut to the chase, and think very carefully before you answer. If you answer truthfully I will look on you favourably, but if you try and deceive me things will end very badly for you, very badly indeed."

Ted massaged his eyes and focused on the face that was looking at him over the backrest of the front seat. It was a cold, hard, emotionless face that filled Ted with a sense of dread, but he was not afraid, a little scared perhaps but not afraid – he had lived too long to be pushed around by bullies, even if they were evil entities from another dimension.

"Ah, well it's like this. Are you the police? If you are, shouldn't you show me your warrant card or something?"

Vynce fought to maintain his calm.

"No, I am not anything so mundane as the police. I am Vincent Di-Ablo, who until a few minutes ago was on course to be your lord and master. Now tell me, where are the others, before I lose my patience and do something you will regret."

Ted scratched his bristly chin.

"Others? There is only me and my friend here, and as you are not the police I can tell you we were out doing a bit of poaching, you know, catching rabbits or a pheasant or two when these little guys here stopped us and after that it is a little blurry."

Vynce looked at the human trapped in the back seat and knew that he was lying, but before he could answer, Jed, who was still a little fuddled from the lamp's fumes, lunged at Vynce. "Don't tell him anything, Ted, just name, rank and serial number."

Vynce batted off the attack and signalled to his driver who started the engine and pulled the car out of the layby and steered it down the lane towards High Meadow Manor.

In the Land Rover, Emma looked at the screen and accelerated towards the place where Ted and Jed were being held. Their position had been stationary for a moment or two but now the screen showed them moving off in the direction of the manor. She pressed the accelerator further into the carpet and saw the distance between the two blips on the screen narrow. Any moment now they would be within sight.

Peering over the steering wheel, the chauffer of the Bentley gradually became aware of a shadow approaching at speed in his rear view mirror. He squeezed the accelerator and the car sped away, increasing the gap between the two. Had this been a long straight road, the Bentley would have easily outpaced the car behind it, but this was a narrow winding country road and he soon had to brake heavily to get around the bends in the road. He had made it safely around two bends courtesy of the car's traction control system and the skin of his teeth, but the third proved too much for his inadequate driving skills and the car's electronic systems waved a white flag and surrendered to the laws of physics. As he braked, the back of the car slid on some damp leaves and it spun out of control, crashing head on into one of the many trees that lined the road.

Emma jumped on the brakes and the Land Rover skidded to a halt on the road next to the wreckage of the Bentley.

"Are you all right?"

Ted gripped Freddy's hand and extricated himself from the rear seat of the car and climbed out through the smashed window followed shortly afterwards by Jed. During the crash they had been cushioned from the worst of the impact by their Piskie captors, who were surprisingly soft and had acted like airbags, absorbing most of the force of the impact. The Piskies in turn were remarkably resilient and had, apart from a bit of bruising here and there, survived unscathed and were now busy disentangling themselves from the wreckage of the car.

Emma looked at the open passenger door. "Did any of you see where Vynce went?"

Sally finished checking that her two trusted employees had escaped unharmed. She felt guilty that she had got them involved in this mess and potentially risked their lives. Happy that they were none the worse for their ordeal, she gave them both a big hug.

After searching the wreckage of the mangled Bentley and the immediate area, Emma was sure that Vynce was no longer in the vicinity and had probably headed back to the Manor. Reaching into the Land Rover, she removed her phone from its cradle on the dashboard and swiped the screen until she saw the app she was looking for. The icon had the image of a demonic face with devils horns protruding from its head; she selected the app and waved the phone around the open passenger door of the Bentley. After a while a small green dot started to flash on the screen and the words "TARGET ACQUIRED" displayed in big red letters, she then waved her phone in the direction of the open countryside, the dot started to flash again, but this time the screen also showed a direction arrow and compass bearing. The app was a purpose-made tracker built into the phones issued by the organisation to its agents in the field. It could detect and track demonic activity quite accurately over the range of a few hundred metres. The signal was strong so he was not far away and as suspected he was headed back in the direction of the manor.

The mood in the Land Rover was quiet and subdued as they headed down the road to the Manor. Emma had tried to dissuade the others from coming with her as this was her fight now and not theirs, but they were determined to see this through to the end, arguing that they were in too deep to back out now.

The manor was quiet and deserted as he made his way through the entrance of Di-Ablo Enterprises and up the stairs to his office. Terrence was still unconscious in the canteen blissfully unaware of how the evening's events had unfolded, the Piskies however had come to the conclusion that they were on the losing side of the game and had packed up their meagre belongings and were now hitchhiking back to their old life on the Cornish moors.

As he entered his office he was surprised to see a figure dressed in black robes sitting at the conference table. The figure looked up from the crystal ball.

"They are coming for you."

Vynce looked at Dora, the only ally he could depend on in his time of crisis. Her commitment to the cause was well known among his fellow demons; she was someone he could trust. "Yes, Dora, I know. I need to get away for a while, back to the other space to plan my next move. Can you get your ladies together and meet me at the stone circle so they can send me back through?"

Dora shifted uncomfortably in her chair.

"I am afraid we have lost them from the fight. If the truth be told, most of them were just in it for something to do on the long cold winter nights, or to get them out the house and join in with the spirit of the sisterhood. Tonight's experience has made them realise that this is for real and they have gone running back to the safety of their mundane, normal lives. As I say, they are lost to us now. But I am still your humble servant and will do what I can to get you away from here so that your power might rise once more."

Vynce nodded. From this side of the dimensional plane he could use the emergency incantations and open the portal himself, but as he performed the ritual he would be vulnerable to those that wished him harm. The ladies of the coven could have given him some protection while he transitioned from this realm. No matter, this was the hand he had been dealt and Dora was an experienced occult practitioner who he could trust to cover his back.

"That is inconvenient, but with you on my side I am sure we can do without them. Collect anything you need and we will head out to the stone circle."

Stopping the Land Rover in the shadows a little way away from the offices of Di-Ablo Enterprises, Emma briefly remembered the first time she had walked through the doors and her encounter with the slightly eccentric receptionist. In contrast to that bright sunny morning, the building was now eerily quiet and in darkness. As they approached the front door the silence was suddenly broken by the sound of what seemed to be a blunt chainsaw struggling to cut its way through a very thick hardwood tree. Emma raised her arm in a signal for them to stop and take cover. After a while the noise stopped and they were once again plunged into the depths of silence.

Jed looked at Emma.

"What was that? Could it be Vynce calling up some of his demonic mates?"

"I am not sure. You wait here while I go and investigate."

"No chance. If you go, we all go. I am not waiting here to be picked off by another one of his diabolical henchmen."

There was a murmur of agreement and the band from Rose Well Farm moved cautiously through the front door and into the reception area. As they worked their way through the building, they passed the entrance to the canteen. Just as Emma poked her head around the door to check all was clear, the chainsaw started up again, this time louder than ever, and instinctively she jumped back into the relative safety of the corridor. After regaining her composure, she cautiously poked her head around the door for a second time and looked back into the room to see the prone figure of Terrence on the floor snoring away in his drink-induced slumber. Relieved that they had found the source of the unnerving sound and realising that Terrence was no longer a threat to them, they continued to make their way cautiously up the stairs towards Vynce's office.

The room was empty; there was no sign of Vynce either in his office or the conference room. Emma fished her phone out of her pocket and stabbed at the screen with her finger. The green dot once again started to flash on the display, and this time the dot was stronger and brighter than before. She adjusted some filters on the app and the strong green dot slowly split into two slightly fainter dots. Vynce had company. She fiddled with the app settings again to show the direction and distance information on the screen.

"Vynce has left the building and is heading to some open ground on the edge of the manor grounds. Is there anything of significance there?"

Ted scratched at his stubbly chin and thought for a second. He had lived his whole life in the village and knew every house, road, field, and footpath in the area.

"I can only think of the old stone circle. It's on the edge of the village and is where the local witches coven gathers from time to time to practice their rituals. It's quite harmless, just a bit of fun. My aunt used to go there to get away from my uncle for a bit of peace and a chat with her friends. She finds the damp plays havoc with her arthritis now so she stays at home and watches the telly instead."

Emma opened the mapping app on her phone, zoomed in on the stone circle and checked the description. According to the information on the screen the stone circle was an active portal to the demonic dimension, albeit a low energy one that could only be accessed by the more powerful demonic entities, and as such was not on their priority watch list.

Unfortunately Vynce was more than powerful enough to

open the portal; the question was, did he intend to disappear back to his own dimension or was he going to use the person he had with him to help him transport others into this dimension to bolster his evil intent to conquer the world.

"I think it may be a bit more serious now. We need to stop him before he reaches the circle, which is the fastest way?"

Things were a little snug on the backseat of the Land Rover as it bounced its way across the open parkland of High Meadow Manor towards the stone circle on the edge of the village. Emma was driving and Sally had taken the front passenger seat, so Freddy was now sandwiched between Ted and Jed on the backseat, all three men flailing about as the off-roader raced at what Freddy thought was an unreasonable speed across the open countryside.

"Why the hurry? If as you say the stone circle is a gateway to another dimension, surely it makes sense to let him go back to his own dimension leaving us to get back on with our own mundane lives."

Raising her voice over the serious squeaking and rattling noises that were coming out of the aging off-roader's chassis and suspension, Emma did her best to put down the rebellion that she felt was fermenting in the back seat.

"Hopefully that is his intention, but there is the possibility that he might use the power of the stone circle to bring through a small army of loyal demons in an attempt to consolidate his power here on earth. If that is the case we must intercept him and take him into custody before he reaches it."

Freddy did not like what he was hearing, the thought of taking Vynce into custody sounded quite suicidal so despite the violent bucking of the Land Rover he did his best to sit back and contemplate his fate. If the ride across the open parkland didn't get him, he was sure that Vynce would.

Standing in the circle, Vynce looked around the standing stones and thought back to that time long ago when he had stood in the same spot, fresh out of Hell's premier academic college. He had been young and idealistic, if not a little naive. It had been only his second outing among the humans and he remembered how they had chased him across the fields, pitchforks and flaming flambeaus in hand until they had trapped him in this very spot, encircling him, some waving crosses at him in a futile attempt to diminish his power.

It had been an act of self-defence, the mob has wished him harm, at the time it seemed the only course of action. He could still remember it now after all this time, standing his ground defiantly as the crowd moved in, he raised his arms to the heavens and shouted out loudly and clearly the sacred words. The crowd stopped as if frozen in time, then a fraction of a second later there had been an enormous sonic boom that had frightened even him, then silence. After that he remembered the feeling of smug satisfaction as he looked around and saw that the angry mob that had once surrounded him were now pillars of stone. That was many centuries ago and if in the same situation again he would now do things differently, as such things were frowned upon these days, even in his dimension. How he missed those simpler times.

Creeping stealthily through the darkness towards the stone circle, Freddy could feel the dampness from the night's dew seeping through the cuffs of his trousers into his socks and by a process of osmosis down into his shoes, making him feel uncomfortable and longing for the warmth of his bed. He was just about to voice his opinion when the group in front of him stopped and crouched down. He followed their lead.

"What's going on? Can we call this off as I am cold wet and hungry?"

Emma signalled for him to be quiet.

"There he is. It looks like he is about to open the portal. Now you stay here, I am going into the circle to try and stop him. If this goes wrong, get out of here and inform them back at headquarters what has gone on here tonight."

Standing in the stone circle facing the two large upright stones, Vynce raised his arms to the heavens and started to recite the ancient sacred incantation. As he spoke, a breeze started to blow around the stones and a slow, low-frequency buzzing began to emanate from them.

Also in the circle with her back to Vynce stood Dora, concentrating her mind into the crystal ball that now stood on the alter stone. As she looked into the crystal she could see the life forces of the group crouched in the shadows waiting to stop her and her master. She made an incantation of her own and projected an energy wave towards them.

As she stood up, Emma could feel the anti-supernatural energy necklace that she, Sally and Freddy were wearing to ward off any evil intent start to get warm as the central turquoise stone started to glow. Good, she thought, the device was working, it would protect her from any evil force that was sent in her direction, so she stood up and started to advance on the two figures in the stone circle.

Dora, sensing that the spell was not working, increased the power from the crystal to the maximum level she could muster on her own. Emma felt the necklace get uncomfortably hot as the power directed against her increased, but the necklace was doing its job and she was protected against the spell. She continued onwards.

Realising that the spell was useless against the woman who was advancing menacingly towards her, Dora changed tack and concentrated all of her life energy into the crystal to form a dome of energy around the perimeter of the stone circle to protect them as Vynce went about the task of opening the portal. As hard as she tried, Emma could not break through the energy field; every time she tried her body was zapped with what seemed to her to be a high voltage charge that fried every nerve in her body and drained her energy until she fell in a heap on the ground unable to move.

Inside the protective dome, Vynce was finishing his incantation. The buzzing from the stones had risen to an uncomfortable level that vibrated the very fibres of his corporeal body, until just as he thought he could not take any more, purple sparks tracked between the two large upright stones and a small plywood door marked "EMERGENCY EXIT" appeared between them. It was not as grand as the door that the coven had conjured up on his arrival, but it was his way out, his route to freedom. He grabbed the handle, opened it and stepped through.

Feeling her energy waning, Dora turned around in time to see Vynce disappearing into the black void beyond the door. Instinctively she staggered towards the opening and followed Vynce in to wherever it was he had gone. Through the haze of the doorway she could see Emma pick herself up off the floor and get unsteadily back on her feet. The protective energy dome was now dissipating and Emma had no difficulty entering the stone circle and headed towards the still-open portal. Dora slammed the door shut behind her and slid the bolt across. In the stone circle the door slowly faded from reality and the silence of the night once again returned to blot out the memory of the events that had occurred just a few moments before.

Chapter Fourteen

In the stone circle Emma surveyed the scene. The portal had disappeared along with Vynce and Dora, the only evidence that something strange had happened there that night was a slight whiff of ozone in the air and the crystal ball that stood passively on the alter stone.

She picked up the crystal ball and joined the rest of the group who were making their way back to the car, happy in the knowledge of a job well done.

A new dawn broke over the world. It was a different one to the new dawn that had been envisaged by Vynce Di-Ablo. The day he had planned as the day where he would take his place as the ruler of the world had been replaced by business as usual. The peoples of the world awoke largely unaware of what had happened during the night and carried on with their daily routines safe in their ignorance.

At Rose Well Farm the new dawn was being met by the smell of frying bacon and freshly brewed coffee. Freddy was busy in the kitchen making bacon sandwiches for everyone while Sally busied herself pouring the coffee into large mugs. It had been a hectic and exhausting night and all those sat around the kitchen table felt tired and hungry, to which bacon sandwiches and coffee seemed the perfect antidote.

Emma picked up a sandwich, added a generous helping of brown source and took a bite. It tasted good, and along with the mug of strong coffee that Sally had just handed to her she could feel her sagging energy levels rise a little. She had just come off the phone from headquarters after a preliminary debriefing on the night's events – all had gone well if not totally as planned. Vynce had retreated back to his own realm and his plot had been foiled, the fire at the barn had destroyed all of the drums of stolen nerve agent, and operatives from a shadowy government department were at the moment removing all the stock of "Di-Ablo's Revenge" from the warehouse at High Meadow Manor and taking it away to a secret facility for analysis. A warning was being issued to the stockist and the public that the Di-Ablo brand of cider had been contaminated and that all bottles should be returned to the supplier with immediate effect.

At High Meadow Manor, Terrence had been woken by the sounds of many human boots crunching on the gravel outside the window of the canteen. The sound reverberated around the inside of his head like claps of thunder. As quietly as he could muster, he made his way out of the emergency exit and avoiding the humans he slowly made his way back to his barn, muttering oaths under his breath about the Piskies and their moonshine apple brandy. As he approached his barn he was shocked and saddened at the sight of the charred and still smouldering remains of what once had been the nerve agent store, but more importantly had also been his home. He flopped down onto the stump of an ancient oak tree and took in the enormity of the situation: all his friends had gone, disappeared in the night while he was sleeping, and on top of all that he had lost the best job he ever had, and was now homeless. He sat there for a moment pondering his fate, before getting back on his feet and starting to walk in a westerly direction, skirting around the activities of the humans. He would go to Cornwall and stay with the piskies for a while until he got back on his feet. From the tales they used to tell around the camp fire at night, Cornwall was a land of legendary giants so it stood to reason there would a place for a being of his stature to make a living in that part of the world.

Sitting at the table in one of the dimension's chicer bistros, Dora sipped at what she had been told was this dimension's version of coffee. She looked around unsure of what to make of her new surroundings. It would take a while to get used to them, although to be fair it was not that different from where she had just come from, apart from it was very hot, the sky was red and there was a distinctive smell of sulphur in the air. These things apart, it still had the same sort of structure as what she now referred to as the old country, with houses, roads, shops, bars and cafes, and a hierarchical system of society, it was just that everything was just that bit eviler, including the coffee she was drinking. As she sat there sipping her evil witches' brew and looking out of the window, she could see some of history's more notorious characters, corrupt politicians, gangsters and dictators going about their daily business. It seemed that here, like in her old dimension, if you sold your soul to the right people you would get yourself a better life. The one thing though that she could not get used to was the omnipresent sound of the wailing of souls that were in continuous torment. The sound was everywhere, day and night, indoors and outdoors, it ground into every fibre of her being and was slowly wearing her down, and although she had a privileged position here as a friend of Vynce Di-Ablo she felt she needed to get back home to the old country.

She took a sip of her brew and turned to Vynce who was busy plotting his next scheme to enslave humanity with a coffee that could control people's minds. He figured that humans were already addicted to coffee so with a few tweaks here and there it should be a relatively simple job to manipulate the formula and get them into accepting him as their supreme leader. After all, what could go wrong!

"Vynce, I think I have got it. We have been going about this the wrong way, instead of using a blunt instrument like your psychotropic cider, or your new coffee blend to enslave humanity, we need to be a bit stealthier and play a longer game. How about if we retune the portal to bring us out in the latter years of the twentieth century and use your power and influence to set up a social media company, that way we can slowly gather a large worldwide following that touches the lives of everyone on the planet, from the lowest peasant to the leaders of governments. Then once your brand has become interwoven in the fabric of everyone's daily life we will have them where we want them and we can then covertly take over with the minimum amount of effort and without arousing suspicion. I doubt if they will even realise."

Vynce stopped what he was doing, scratched his head and pondered the idea for a while. "That is an intriguing notion, please, go on and tell me more."